Praise for Julie Leto's *STRIPPED,* winner of
the *Romantic Times BOOKreviews*
Best Blaze of 2007 Award

"Fresh characters, perfect details, passionate
relationships, humor and sizzling sex
all make this novel a winner."
—*Romantic Times BOOKreviews*

"I really loved the chemistry between the leads.
I loved the magic, the secondary characters and
the action, and I cannot wait for the next one!"
—*New York Times* bestselling author
Gena Showalter

"This was my first read by Julie Leto, and it
won't be my last. It satisfied on every level:
good romance, good sex, good action."
—*The Good, The Bad and The Unread*

"Sexy, sassy, and fun, *Stripped* by Julie Leto
is one book designed to make your summer
exciting and a whole lot hotter."
—*Cataromance*

Blaze

Dear Reader,

Anyone who's been reading Harlequin Blaze for a while has probably noticed that the heroines in our line are...um, different from ordinary women. Okay, they're different from *me*. But I believe a Blaze heroine is the woman I *want* to be, even when my career, my family, or my day-to-day responsibilities keep me from grabbing life by the lapels and saying, "I've done it your way long enough...it's my turn now."

I've built a career writing heroines who are one step to the left (or right!) of center and the delicious, confident, sexy men who love them. But once in a while a woman drifts into my imagination who is kind of ordinary...in an off-beat way. Such a woman is Josie Vargas, who first appeared as a secondary character in my August 2007 Blaze novel, *Stripped*. Josie proved to be a free-spirited anchor for Rick Fernandez, a once steady, by-the-book cop whose life has turned upside down. Now he's hunting down the evilest of the evil, and without Josie's intervention (and more important, her love) he might just go down a path from which there is no return.

Something Wicked is the final story in my St. Lyon witches series, which started with the novella "Under His Spell" in the *Witchy Business* anthology, then continued with *Stripped*. There are also appearances by characters featured in my novella "Driven to Distraction" from the *A Fare To Remember* collection. I love revisiting characters, and I hope you enjoy it, as well!

Happy reading,

Julie

Julie Leto

SOMETHING WICKED

HARLEQUIN®

TORONTO • NEW YORK • LONDON
AMSTERDAM • PARIS • SYDNEY • HAMBURG
STOCKHOLM • ATHENS • TOKYO • MILAN • MADRID
PRAGUE • WARSAW • BUDAPEST • AUCKLAND

Recycling programs
for this product may
not exist in your area.

ISBN-13: 978-0-373-79452-2
ISBN-10:   0-373-79452-5

SOMETHING WICKED

Copyright © 2009 by Julie Leto Klapka.

www.eHarlequin.com

Printed in U.S.A.

ABOUT THE AUTHOR

New York Times and *USA TODAY* bestselling author Julie Leto has a reputation for writing ultrasexy, edgy stories, despite (or maybe because of) her previous profession as a Catholic high school teacher. Born and raised in sunny Florida, Julie lives in Tampa with her husband, daughter, a very spoiled dachshund and the world's largest guinea pig. For more information on Julie's books, check out www.julieleto.com or visit and chat with her at the popular blog site www.plotmonkeys.com.

Books by Julie Leto

This one is for my sister-in-law, Jeannette Leto, because even though she's never really gotten a character named after her, my heroines keep staying in "her" apartment. One of these days, this jet-setter is going to show up in a book and I promise, "you" will be just as fictionally fabulous as you are for real.

1

RICK PUNCHED Josie Vargas's number into his cell phone. He'd only dialed the seven digits twice since he'd met her, but the sequence flowed from his memory, with a bit of a melody behind it, as if he'd memorized it with the music like the alphabet song. Their first real date, just last night, had been incredibly ordinary and ultimately fantastic. Dinner. A movie. Talking. Lots and lots of talking.

And then, the kissing.

Lots and lots of kissing.

He'd had to harness every ounce of his self-control not to try and seduce her out of her clothes the moment they'd stepped into her apartment. Not an easy task for either of them, but they'd managed to remain upright and fully dressed.

Damn it.

They weren't teenagers. And clearly, both of them knew a good thing when they saw it. So they'd disentangled from each other with a promise to take things slowly.

Get to know each other.

Become friends first.

Good thing they lived in Chicago, where cold showers were cheap and easy to come by.

Rick hit the Talk button on his phone, then adjusted the crotch of his slacks as he walked away from the office building where he'd just engaged in an unauthorized and unwise operation with his former boss. He'd much rather think about Josie. Her silky hair. Her soulful eyes. Her curvy, sensitive breasts. Thinking about her got him hard as a rock, which made it so much easier to forget just how many rules he'd broken in the past twenty-four hours and how, in all likelihood, his career was about to nose-dive into a backed-up toilet.

Might not be so bad with Josie around. She certainly made all the other parts of his life a lot more interesting.

Rick hadn't been the same since the moment she'd literally run into him at the precinct. She'd been searching for her best friend, Lilith St. Lyon, the department's on-call psychic. Since Rick had been trained from birth by his Cuban-American mother and his equally old-school sisters to socialize only with women who would someday make a good wife, he might not have noticed her otherwise. Her blond, sun-streaked hair, hippy-dippy tunic, long skirt and lace-up sandals put her in the "do not touch" category. And yet, he'd been intrigued.

She broke every rule his *familia* had laid out.

Good, preferably Latino family?

Her last name was Vargas, so she had a Latin connection, but every member of her family came with a rap sheet.

Catholic?

Ha! Wiccan.

Loves children?

He hadn't yet garnered her opinion on *niños* or *niñas,* but she'd hinted that her crazy childhood hadn't left her unscarred.

Adores cooking and cleaning and tending to her man's every need?

Again, Rick chuckled. He could certainly imagine Josie preferring to live her life barefoot, but pregnant and in the kitchen? Never in a million years.

Of course, his family wasn't stuck entirely in the previous

century. They also wanted Rick's future wife (as any and all girlfriends were considered to be) to have an advanced degree from college so that she could, if necessary, support the family should Rick's career in law enforcement come to a violent end. But as far as he knew, Josie had graduated exclusively from the school of hard knocks. And while her career as a shopkeeper seemed successful enough, her business selling custom aromatherapy candles and pagan paraphernalia was firmly entrenched in a coveted location on Chicago's Magnificent Mile. There would be no moving to Miami once the kidlets arrived, as was expected.

The perfect woman she was not.

And yet, Rick couldn't get her out of his mind.

"In the mood for pizza?" he asked after she finally answered the phone with a breathless hello that made his skin dance with a shamefully electric thrill.

"Deep-dish?"

The relief in her voice was unmistakable and incredibly appealing. She knew he'd been on the job tonight. She'd been worried, too. And as much as he didn't want to cause her any anxiety, he liked the idea that she cared.

Liked it a lot.

"Is there any other kind of pizza in this town?"

"Want to go out or order in?"

"In," Rick said instantly, then caught the eagerness in his voice. After the make-out session they'd shared last night, he didn't want Josie thinking he just wanted to get her into bed. Even if he did. Badly. "Unless you want to go out."

Josie hummed shyly. "I'm okay with either. Let's decide after you get here. How'd everything go? Are Mac and Lilith with you?"

Rick glanced back at the service door he'd used to exit the office building, expecting his former boss and his lover to appear at any moment. He hadn't wanted to tell Josie about tonight's operation. Hell, he hadn't wanted to take part in the interrogation in the first place. He wasn't a stickler for every single rule in the law enforcement handbook, but he did have limits. And tonight, nearly every single one had been pushed to the breaking point.

If Mac Mancusi hadn't been the one asking for his help, Rick would have refused. Mac had been chief of detectives in the Chicago P.D. since Rick joined the unit. Though Mac had been suspended from the job a few days ago for pissing off the mayor, he was still Rick's friend. Rick trusted him implicitly—even after he'd come to him with a story that might have made a great feature film. A mutually hated defense attorney had supposed ties to a massive drug shipment their sources reported was about to hit the streets. Believable enough. But then Mac had added in the possibility that the well-connected lawyer was also, possibly, a warlock.

Cue the creepy soundtrack.

And yet, Rick had still listened. Lilith St. Lyon had backed up Mac's outlandish suspicions and though she was a little woo-woo herself, she'd never steered Rick wrong, even if she did scare the crap out of him. He'd grown up in Little Havana and while he had a healthy respect for the *brujas* and *santeros,* he certainly didn't subscribe to their ways. The one and only time he'd met his maternal great-grandmother, a woman whose Sight had reportedly once caught the attention of Fidel Castro, Rick had been freaked out enough to never want to visit his parents' homeland again. When Lilith, a psychic, had asked Rick to be a conduit through which she could listen in on his interrogation of Boothe Thompson, the defense attorney suspected in the murder of a low-level drug dealer, Rick had reluctantly agreed. The ends justified the means. And he wasn't six years old and in a foreign country anymore.

But they'd learned nothing new. Before Rick had left the building and called Josie, Mac and Lilith had been right behind him.

"Maybe they came out in the front," he said, more to himself than to Josie.

He started walking as he told her more than he should about their operation. He'd already fractured just about every department regulation tonight by conspiring with a suspended officer to interrogate a respected defense attorney. Telling Josie the outcome wasn't going to get him any more fired.

"We got nothing," he admitted. "The man is slippery. I didn't think we'd get him to fess up to anything, and I was right."

"And Lilith couldn't sense anything?" she asked.

While Rick asked the questions, Mac and Lilith had been in a nearby room, listening in through a psychic connection Rick didn't even try to understand. But Lilith hadn't discovered anything they could use to connect Thompson to the murder of the dealer or the impending drug shipment.

"Nothing we could use," he admitted, gulping down his frustration.

For as long as he could remember, Rick had wanted to be a cop. He'd finished high school a year early, studied criminal justice in college and joined the Miami-Dade department before he was twenty-one. Known for his efficient, cool and reasoned thinking, he'd moved up quickly to detective. After five years of an endless battle against the influx of drugs in Miami, he'd moved to Chicago, hoping to broaden his knowledge base. Deal with crimes that weren't always about smack, crack and pot. But now, he was back where he didn't want to be—in the middle of yet another drug war, one that was being influenced by someone very powerful and, as of yet, very unknown.

"And what did it feel like, having Lilith use you that way?" Josie asked. "Was it cool?"

The fascination in her voice made him chuckle and forget how the whole setup had initially unnerved him. As a cop, he was used to dealing with hunches, and he'd always guessed that Lilith just had better hunches than most. In Little Havana, however, he'd met a few *brujas,* like his great-grandmother in Cuba, whose insight had been downright scary. A witch in Miami had predicted his father's heart attack only days before he'd been felled by a cardiac episode that should have killed him. But because of the witch, he'd put an aspirin in his pocket—and that little pill had saved his life.

"It was freaky," he admitted. "I could sense that she was there, listening in. At one point, she even suggested that I ask a certain question and I just—"

Rick, help us.

What the hell?

He pulled the phone away from his ear. A few people strode beside him on the sidewalk with heads down and strides swift. At the curb, a driver leaned lazily against a stretch limousine, tapping into his iPhone. Rick peered into the office building's lobby. No sign of Mac or Lilith, even though he could have sworn he just heard her voice.

"Rick? Rick, are you there?"

Tinny and distant, Josie's voice echoed from the phone, which he lifted back to his ear.

"Yeah," he confirmed. "I just—"

Rick, please. Hear me. He's not a warlock. The mayor is. Thompson's a witch. Black magic. He'll kill us.

"Just what? Rick, what's wrong?"

He shook his head, but the crowded feeling in his mind didn't lessen. Lilith was invading his consciousness, but this time, she was calling for help.

He stopped walking and turned. He spied the plates on the limousine. City government issue. The mayor?

At that moment, the driver spared him a glance. Rick gave a nod, then turned and cursed. "It's Lilith. She's connected to me again. They're in trouble. He's going to kill them. He's a witch, and he's using black magic."

Josie gasped. "Can you—"

"Yes," Rick said, "I've got to go."

"Be—"

He snapped the phone shut. He didn't need Josie's warning. For the benefit of the limo driver, he strode casually back down the sidewalk, but broke into a run and yanked out his firearm once he cleared the side of the building. If Lilith had called for help, she and Mac were in deep. Witches? Warlocks? Black magic? This was all too fucking weird, but he had to try and help. He couldn't leave them to die.

He'd used a service door to exit the building, but it had locked automatically behind him. If he tried the front entrance and alerted security or the mayor's driver, all hell could break loose. Demanding instant cooperation from his frazzled brain, Rick spotted a ratty cushion protruding from a nearby Dumpster. He grabbed it, placed it over the unyielding knob and fired his weapon into the lock, muffling the sound as best he could. For a split second, he considered calling for backup, but this had been an unauthorized operation from the start. Rick had helped Mac out of loyalty, out of trust. The backlash against both of them could ruin their careers forever. He'd trust Mac a little while longer. His suspension notwithstanding, Mac was a good cop. And a good friend.

As Rick dashed into the elevator, he closed his eyes and thought hard, trying to communicate to Lilith that he was on his way. He felt her screaming just before the elevator reached the floor he somehow knew she was on. As the doors slid open, he saw her standing across from the recently elected mayor of Chicago, whose hands sparked with electricity that swirled before his eyes and formed into a stunning lethal ball.

Rick couldn't speak. He couldn't move. No one had noticed the elevator, but when the doors started to close, he instinctively stepped out and stood, motionless, unable to fully comprehend what he was seeing. The defense attorney, Boothe Thompson lay motionless and empty-eyed at the mayor's feet. When Mac drew his gun, the mayor shifted and waved his sparking hand. The gun flew across the hallway. Mac dove to retrieve the weapon and before Rick could act, Lilith plunged forward, the glint of her knife flashing only a split second before it disappeared inside the mayor's chest.

Then, they both crumpled to the ground. The mayor, dead, and Lilith…? Rick shouted at Mac, who turned and saw Lilith on the floor. He screamed her name and flew to her side.

Rick stepped forward, but was stopped by a dark shadow that poured out of the mayor's eye sockets and mouth, then surrounded Rick like a wool blanket in July. Itchy. Hot. Smothering.

Take me in, human.

The voice pounded hard against Rick's skull, as if demanding entrance. The excruciating pain stole Rick's eyesight and squeezed his trachea shut. The chain he wore around his neck tightened and the crucifix at the end burned. He dropped to his knees. His gun thumped to the ground beside him.

I am not through with this world, the voice continued, cutting into Rick's ears, stabbing at his brain. *So young. So powerful,* it expressed lustily. *Your rewards will be endless.*

A million jumbled thoughts exploded in Rick's mind. Images of decadence, luxury, power and limitless freedom splayed before him, a grand temptation to someone who had not been forewarned.

But Rick had heard his great-grandmother, even if her

prophecy when he was six had gifted him with a lifetime of nightmares.

You will fight a great evil who will offer you everything you've ever wanted, she'd said in Spanish. *But only you can resist him,* niño. *Only you can destroy him.*

Rick concentrated on the memory, holding on to it like a lifeline, fixing the image of his *bisabuela's* rheumy blue eyes, kind toothless grin and the saint's medal she'd clutched in her hand as she spoke. Fire exploded in his chest and a scream of anguish unlike any he'd ever heard burst through his ear-drums. The pounding in his head intensified, nearly knocking him unconscious as the shadow tightened around him then, in a flash, dispersed. Behind him, the dark entity slid into the cracks of the elevator door and disappeared.

Rick gulped in the cool air as his eyes adjusted, allowing light to penetrate where moments before, there had been only darkness. As he struggled, he had the irresistible urge to throw himself into the nearest steaming hot shower to wash away the filth that seemed crusted, invisible, to his skin.

Grabbing blindly, he found his firearm and attempted to stand. He lifted his weapon, but just as Mac's had, the gun shot out of his grip, landing in the hands of a regal, dark-haired woman dressed entirely in purple. She had materialized directly in his path.

"I mean you no harm," she said calmly.

Rick threw himself back against the elevator doors. "What just happened to me? Who the hell are you?"

"I'm Regina St. Lyon, Lilith's sister and Guardian of Witches. Josie called me. I'm here to help."

She spun away from Rick and immediately slid to the floor beside Lilith and Mac.

"What's wrong with her?" Mac asked.

Regina passed her hand over Lilith's face. "She's unconscious. I believe she overloaded psychically when she touched the warlock. Take her out of here, Mac. Get her someplace safe."

"But what about—" said Rick.

Regina stood. "I'll take care of this situation, Detective, but the evil vibrations still linger here. She needs a healing place. Please."

Mac scooped Lilith into his arms and dashed toward the elevator. Rick pushed the button. The doors swung immediately open.

"Help her," Mac said, nodding his head toward Regina. "She'll need you to fix this."

The doors closed and Rick turned to see Regina surveying the two dead bodies, shattered glass and scorch marks in the hallway with all the calculated coolness of a well-trained crime-scene analyst. He gasped, suddenly realizing he hadn't taken in enough oxygen. Stars shot through his vision, and he had to grasp the wall to keep from stumbling.

When he righted himself, he caught Regina staring at him with eyes the color of purple gemstones.

"Tell me what happened here," she demanded.

Her superior tone snapped him out of his fugue, but he had no doubt that she was one of *them*. Not human. Not normal.

"Two people died," he answered curtly.

She arched a careless brow. "I observed as much. But I need you to point to the evidence that proves how they died."

Clearly, she had no idea that he'd been attacked seconds before her arrival by a shadow that had emerged from the dead mayor's body. And he wasn't about to tell her. Had he imagined the whole episode? Had the connection with Lilith cost him his sanity? He'd have suspected Regina, too, was a figment of his imagination if Mac hadn't just spoken with her seconds before.

"Why?" he asked, anticipating an answer he didn't want to hear.

"Do you really need for me to tell you?"

He was a cop. He had to think like a cop. Assess the crime scene. Catalogue the evidence. Formulate a working theory that could be backed up by proof.

Her gaze flicked toward the elevator doors, where Mac and Lilith had just escaped. Mac and Lilith, who would, from the evidence he observed and what he'd seen with his own eyes, be charged if not convicted of a double murder.

Unless he told Regina what she needed to know.

Unless he ignored what had just happened and denied the moral path he'd followed since birth.

Something unexplainable had occurred here. Something evil. Something wicked. But mostly, something unjust. He couldn't allow Mac and Lilith to pay the price. He did as she asked and told her all that he had seen and heard. Then, once she was satisfied that she understood the full breadth of the situation, Regina asked Rick one last question.

"So how do we ensure that neither my sister nor Mac is charged with murder?"

Rick eyed her with a loathing he had not felt in years. She was asking him to help her cover up a crime. It went against everything he'd ever believed in, even before he joined the police force. Justice wasn't supposed to work this way. Was it?

"First," he answered, his chest cracking open with each syllable he uttered, "we get rid of their fingerprints."

2

Six months later...

THERE WAS A TIME when sneaking off to a hotel room with
Rick Fernandez had been Josie's ultimate fantasy. She'd spent
hours in bed at night, mulling over every detail, imagining
every moment. She'd fill the luxury suite of a hotel overlook-
ing Lake Michigan with candles of her own design—candles
that would enhance their senses. The strawberries and chocolate she'd order from room service would burst with sweet
silkiness in their mouths, a prelude to the sugared flavor of
slow, intense kisses. The music she'd tune on the suite's high-
definition stereo would block out any sounds of the city below.
She had even gone to Victoria's Secret at Water Tower Place
and imagined exactly which silk panty or satin bra would
drive Rick utterly mad with desire.

Staring up at the dive motel on the dark edge of East
Harlem in New York City, she wondered how her sexual fantasy had turned into such a nightmare.

Behind her, men in tattered clothes and smelling strongly
of unwashed skin, car exhaust and cheap whiskey, accosted
a pair of prostitutes tottering past on acrylic heels. The women
ignored the catcalls, but gave Josie a disapproving once-over
as they sidled by. Josie glanced down at her own attire—snug
but comfortable jeans, twin tank tops and a sleek leather

jacket that worked fine to ward off the occasional chill in the unusually warm February air. She was here for seduction, yes, but she was not competing with the area's working girls. She was here for one man and one man only.

Rick.

She'd staked out the hotel earlier. After months of following his ghostlike trail, she'd spotted him just before dawn and had followed him here. One bribe later and she'd acquired the number to his hotel room. She had to hope and pray that while she'd formulated her plan, he hadn't left. Holding tight to a can of pepper spray in her pocket, she slipped into the alley and, once certain no one was around, jimmied the side door so she could enter without alerting anyone in the lobby. In the minutes just before nightfall, the place was fairly deserted. The hookers hadn't yet shown up with their johns and the drug addicts weren't yet sober enough to go out to find their next fix.

But Rick was here. He had to be. She'd been searching for months, ever since he'd disappeared the night Lilith and Mac had been attacked by the mayor. She'd heard from him only once, in a note she'd found hidden in the cash register at her shop, telling her goodbye.

The fact that he thought she'd leave matters alone on account of the contents of one scribbled note verified how little he knew her. Something had happened that night—something neither Mac nor Lilith nor Regina, the Guardian of Witches who had approved Josie's search, knew about. Something that had sent Rick deep underground.

She'd encouraged him to help Mac and Lilith that night. She couldn't help bearing some of the responsibility for the aftermath. But that wasn't why she was here. The drive to find Rick after he'd gone missing stemmed from emotions she'd never felt before. She believed in Fate. She ascribed to the whims of Destiny. And yes, she even had faith in love at first sight.

Though it wasn't sight that had drawn her to Rick. She wouldn't deny that he was one of the most handsome men she'd ever encountered, but it took more than a hot guy to turn Josie's head. Rick had a presence that struck her deep within her soul, in the part of her that longed for someone both normal and extraordinary at the same time.

She'd found that with Rick, she was sure. Unfortunately, he didn't feel the same or he never would have gone.

Still, his disappearance left too many questions for her to ignore. On the most basic level, she needed to discover where he was and why he'd put himself into the dangerous, gray and bloody area between the magical and the mundane worlds. But more deeply, she had to know if maybe, under other circumstances, their relationship might have worked out. Too bad she had no idea which question she'd tackle first.

She approached his room cautiously. She wasn't sure exactly what she was going to find on the other side of the pocked and peeling door, but she was about certain there wouldn't be a single scented candle or soft, romantic music. Not in this joint.

"Don't go in there."

Josie yanked her shaking hand away from the doorknob and spun, startled. Unable to move—to even gasp in surprise—she watched Regina St. Lyon emerge from the shadows. Relieved, Josie allowed herself a split second to breathe.

"Oh, it's you."

"So you've found him," Regina said.

"Nice to see you, too," Josie said with a forced smile. She'd hadn't exactly been avoiding contact with the Guardian of Witches, but she wasn't thrilled to see her, either. For the past six months, Rick had been causing a disruption in the division between the mundane and magical worlds. As Guardian, it was Regina's responsibility to find and stop him.

Fortunately for Josie, even Regina's considerable magical prowess did not include the ability to find a nonmagical human who did not want to be found—not and leave him alive. So she'd recruited Josie, giving her six months to accomplish her goal before she took matters into her own hands.

Josie's time was nearly up.

Regina gave a polite bow and grinned. The effect relaxed the deep furrow on her forehead. "You look well."

"I was going for sexy," she answered, tugging her tank tops down a bit lower.

Regina arched a brow. "You plan to seduce him into stopping his rampage?"

"Sounds like a win-win-win for all involved," Josie said with a smile.

While Regina had a tendency to blow up things that annoyed her, Josie believed in a quieter form of magic, particularly since she had no real powers. What could be more peaceful than motivating a man to stop wreaking havoc in the magical world by distracting him with sex?

Regina's smile, however, disappeared. She turned her hand palm up. A ball of pure electricity materialized just above her flesh, then spun. The color, deep purple to match her eyes, was entrancing, but Josie knew the sphere was deadly. She'd never seen Regina use her most formidable weapon, but she'd heard enough to know she couldn't allow Regina and Rick to meet. Not until she'd convinced Rick to give up his apparent quest to destroy all the evil magical beings he could get his hands on.

Not that destroying evil was bad. When Regina had first come to her to solicit her help, Josie had wondered what the problem was. She knew that the Guardian had entire teams of witches training to do exactly what Rick was doing on his own. But he was getting sloppy and if he wasn't stopped, he was going to expose the magical world to the mundane one.

And that wouldn't be good. The Salem witch trials might have happened a few centuries ago, but they were still incredibly fresh in the minds of anyone who practiced Wicca.

Protecting the secrecy of witches was Regina's primary duty. She'd vowed to do whatever she had to in order to keep the magical and mundane worlds from intersecting in a violent way. But about Rick, she was wrong. Josie knew that once she caught up with him, he'd listen to reason. And to present her arguments, first she had to go inside his hotel room.

"I will help him," Josie insisted.

"It's too late," Regina said, her generous lips bowed in a tragic frown.

"You said I had six months. That leaves me one more week."

"I'm not talking about time, Josie. Rick has been dealing with demons too long. He cannot possibly be the same man you knew."

"You don't know that," she argued.

"I know what he has done. His choices—"

"Have served your ultimate purpose. He's destroying your enemies," Josie insisted, hoping to buy a bit more time.

Regina arched a perfectly sculpted eyebrow, her mouth still curved disapprovingly. "I cannot deny that Rick's passion for killing demons has benefited the witching community, but increasingly—" she eyed the door Josie hoped Rick was still behind "—he's becoming a danger to himself and the secrecy of our world. Look how long it has taken you to track him down. His crimes are coming to the attention of mundane law enforcement. Sooner or later, someone will connect him to us and I cannot allow Rick's personal vendetta to expose my Wiccan sisters and brothers, magical or mundane. From this point, you should let us deal with him."

Josie's heart lurched. "What? Now that I led you to New York? To him? Besides, I thought *I* was one of *us?*"

Regina's smile was only partly reassuring. "Mundane witches are the backbone of our community."

"Then why didn't I know you and the others existed until six months ago?"

"Because the knowledge often does more harm than good," Regina insisted, her gaze slashing toward the door. "Look at Rick. Look at what he's become."

"I can't," Josie said, "you're blocking my way."

After a long pause, Regina stepped aside.

Josie had learned about sacred witches like Regina—those who possessed real, active powers—around the same time Rick had, but the idea that such magic existed still boggled her mind. Regina could materialize from nowhere. She had the ability to produce deadly bursts of energy from the palm of her hand. It had been hard enough for Josie to swallow the fact that Lilith St. Lyon, Josie's best friend and Regina's younger sister, was a powerful psychic who'd recently mastered the ability to project her thoughts into the minds of others. And there were other witches out there who could conjure items from nothing, stop time, create doppelgängers and hold sway over the dead. Certainly made Josie's skills with aromatherapy, candles and, to some degree, potions, pale in comparison.

But no matter their magic, none of the witches could find a human who did not want to be found, particularly a former cop with impressive street smarts. Luckily for her, Josie had been raised on those same streets. Her mother, a longtime con, and her various "uncles" of dubious blood relation had taught her a few tricks of her own. Together with finely honed computer skills and the ability to persuade just about anyone to talk to her and give her information they didn't want to share, Josie had finally tracked Rick down. She wasn't going to turn around and hand him over to Regina without giving herself a shot at bringing him home.

"Thank you," Josie said, placing herself firmly in front of Rick's door. "I won't let you down. I won't let Rick down. I promise."

Regina's amethyst eyes narrowed. "This isn't about you, Josie. This is about Rick. You may care about him deeply, even think you love him, but he's descended to a place you might not be able to rescue him from."

Josie lifted her chin defiantly. "I won't accept that."

Regina seemed neither surprised nor dismayed. "Then accept this."

From her pocket, Regina removed a necklace—a green stone flecked with red and set within a gold, heart-shaped charm. She handed it to Josie, who gasped at the instant warmth of the gem against her palm.

"What is this?" she asked, shifting so the dim glow from the single working hallway light washed over the pendant. "A Valentine's Day present?"

Regina snorted. "Guess again."

She pushed aside her impatience to reach Rick and looked down at the necklace a second time, running her finger over the reddish-green stone. "Heliotrope?"

"Very good," Regina complimented.

Josie might not be a sacred witch, but her knowledge of magical herbs and stones was unsurpassed—when she could clear her mind of worry over Rick long enough to think.

"It's also known as bloodstone," Regina went on. "A stone of this quality is very rare and very powerful. We use them for protection."

Josie eyed the Guardian witch warily. "You didn't add a touch of something else, did you?"

"Well, it is nearly Valentine's Day," she replied, a twinkle lightening her unusual eyes.

It was Josie's time to laugh derisively through her nose.

"Last time I checked, the cherub and chocolate holiday was not on the official Wiccan calendar," Josie charged.

Regina grinned. "Not the official one, no. But St. Valentine's feast day is tied to pagan fertility celebrations. And since I now know exactly what you're planning to do to entice Rick back to Chicago…"

"I'm not planning on getting pregnant," Josie reassured her. Quite certain her mother had never intended to be saddled with a child and knowing the aftermath of such carelessness, Josie had been practicing safe sex since she'd lost her virginity. Without exception. She'd use every weapon in her feminine arsenal to entice Rick home to Chicago, but she would never resort to involving an innocent baby.

"Good to hear," Regina said, patting her hand. "But I didn't think you'd go that far. I just know that Wiccan holiday or not, romance is in the air this time of year. Use it to your advantage."

Josie laughed. "That's exactly what I intend to do."

At one time, Josie had doubted she'd ever have even half the self-confidence of either Regina or Lilith. But since meeting Rick—and then losing him before they'd barely had a chance—Josie had tapped into a determination she hadn't felt since she'd left her grifter mother and started her own life in Chicago. So far, the cockiness had served her well. It wasn't magic that would save Rick. It was love.

She held out the necklace. "I don't need amulets or charms. Rick will come back with me in spite of magic, not because of it."

Regina crossed her arms, ignoring Josie's offering. "You think so?"

Josie stepped closer and pushed out her words through a determined mouth. This wasn't the time to show anything but strength. "I'm not your minion, Regina. I don't have to do things your way."

Regina eyed her keenly. "No, you don't. I'm a Guardian, Josie, not a queen. It's my job to protect and defend."

Though Josie had practiced the craft as she'd been taught by her aunt and her grandmother—embracing the power of herbs, scents and stones because they connected her to the Goddess and to Mother Earth—she was just an ordinary woman. She had no real magic. No power beyond her own wits. And from the intense look in the Guardian's eyes, the stakes couldn't be higher.

Josie swallowed thickly and placed the amulet around her neck.

"Rick is a mundane, like me. You're part of the world I suspect he's come to hate, for whatever reason."

"You know the reason," Regina insisted.

Josie shook her head. "Covering up for Mac and Lilith wasn't enough to push him this far. There has to be something more. I'm going to find out what happened. And then, I'm going to bring him home."

"What if you can't?"

Josie sighed. She'd languished over this question every minute of every day since she'd set out to find Rick and stem the rampage he'd been on, hunting and killing the demons and warlocks better left to soldiers in Regina's magical army.

"Lilith told me," Josie admitted, hardly able to speak the psychic's distressing premonition, "that I was the one who had to save him. Right after he disappeared, she tried using her psychic powers to find him and, instead, she saw me. She said if I didn't succeed, he might kill someone who wasn't supposed to die. And then he'd be lost. Forever. I can't fail."

Regina pursed her lips, clearly thinking over all Josie had said. "Lilith's premonitions are terrifyingly accurate, but the future is never written in stone."

She laid her hand on Josie's shoulder, and then stepped

back into the shadows. Her disembodied voice echoed through the dingy hallway and chased a shiver up Josie's spine.

"You have one week. If you can't stop him, we will."

3

ONE WEEK.

One week?

Josie wrapped her arms tightly across her chest and leaned her forehead against the wall. She'd come so far. She wouldn't stop now, not when Rick's life was at stake. Any battle between the Guardian witch and the rogue cop would result in serious casualties. Stretching, she slid her hand, palm flat, against the door, hoping and praying he hadn't escaped while she and Regina argued.

To find him, she'd tapped into skills she'd tried to deny since the day she'd been released from juvie for the last time. Once she was independent-minded enough to realize that her mother's "games" deprived other people of their hard-earned cash and sense of self-worth, Josie had tried to stop the endless stream of cons and grift operations her mother had employed to keep them from living on the streets. But she'd never been strong enough or clever enough to change her mother's chosen way of life. By the time she was a few months away from turning eighteen, Josie had known her chances of a normal childhood had run out.

Determined to at least keep her adult life cleansed of bad karma, Josie had celebrated her birthday by saying *sayonara* to her mother and moving back to Chicago. She took control of valuable real estate left to her by an aunt, opened her store and embraced the Wiccan religion of her grandmother. She'd completely reinvented herself, erasing a past fraught with illegal activity and devoid of hope. If she could accomplish such a transformation alone, then no matter what had happened to Rick to send him into this downward spiral, she knew he could come out of the darkness.

She'd make sure of it.

Revitalized, she tucked the necklace Regina had given her down into her T-shirt. Valentine's Day. For others, it was the holiday of love. For Rick and her, it was D-day.

She knocked on the door, then pressed her ear to the scarred wood to hear if anyone moved inside.

Was that a groan?

She knocked again. "Rick?"

A grunt? Was he hurt?

"Rick!"

She tried the lock. It wouldn't budge. She glanced down the hall, but nixed the option of running for help. The last time she'd hesitated for this long, Rick had eluded her, disappeared with nothing but a barely warm trail in his wake.

She backed up, aimed her foot at the area near the knob and kicked hard.

Pain shot from her heel to her thigh. She hobbled backward, cursing, when a crash sounded beyond the door. Instinct took over. She attacked again and this time, the lock surrendered, the door swung open and Josie toppled into the room.

The smell caught her instantly—the potent sweetness of leather, gun oil and shampoo. And…sage? She bent down to find wilted leaves strewn liberally across the threshold, then followed a trail to another collection beneath the window. Sage protected against evil. That together with the crisp smell of aftershave, the unexpected scent of a man she'd chased through Detroit, Pittsburgh, Boston and now, New York City, brightened her outlook. Maybe he wasn't so lost after all. She clung desperately to her impressions of Rick Fernandez—salt of the earth. Even tempered. Open-minded. And at this moment—passed out.

The grimy windows, shaded by blinds with broken and bent slats, blocked out most of the neon glow from the signs outside. But in the center of the room, on a bed devoid of any covering except for crisp, surprisingly white sheets, lay Rick, facedown and fast asleep.

A clock radio, blinking the midnight hour for likely the last few years, had been knocked to the floor. Appropriate, since time stood still the minute she spotted him on the bed, covered only by a towel. His skin damp, his hair spiked from a shower and an empty bottle of Jack Daniel's clutched in his hand, he was breathtaking.

His dark skin and muscles, which looked hard as stone even in alcohol-induced sleep, made her mouth water. A gold chain cut a contrasting line across his neck, and she imagined that the cross he always wore was tangled somewhere behind his head. They'd only had one real date six months ago and, despite their instant attraction, they'd opted to take things slowly. Now that she'd seen him nearly naked, Josie wondered what kind of a fool of a woman agreed to such a Puritanical condition.

Truth was, from the moment she'd met him, she'd fantasized about Rick naked in bed.

Just not exactly like this.

She shut the door. When she turned back, she gasped. He was sitting up, a gun leveled at her heart, his eyes glazed by a mixture of exhaustion and alarm.

"Rick!"

"Josie?"

She stepped into the dim light streaking in from the window. He scrambled across the bed and snapped on the table lamp.

"Josie."

For a second, she thought she might have heard relief in his voice, but looking at the deep frown on his face, she figured the sound was simply wishful thinking.

With all the will she possessed, she remained rooted to the spot. She had to be smart. Keep her head. Think coolly. Logically. Just like Rick would have. Before.

"Yes, Rick. It's me."

He laid the gun on the mattress but didn't take his hand off the grip. "What are you doing here?"

She pressed her lips together tightly, unsure at first what words would come out of her mouth. Why was she here? Really?

"I came to find you."

He snorted. "Congratulations."

Rick leaned over to the nightstand, exchanged the gun for a package of cigarettes and, finding it empty, threw it, disgusted, onto the floor. Glancing around, Josie doubted this hotel had smoking or nonsmoking designations. She was certain this dump had no maid service, much less the room service she needed to order up a pot of coffee to counteract the slight slur in Rick's speech and the thick red rims around his once bright and shining dark eyes. Only six months ago, he'd been a cop. A detective. Decorated. Respected. Likely well acquainted with man's inhumanity to man and yet, when she'd literally run into him at the police station on the day of her first and only paranormal premonition, his gaze had held a smart optimism that had instantly grabbed Josie's attention.

Now, she saw none of that inner glow. She saw shadows. Anger. A deep, ravaging sadness. Hadn't she expected this? She'd prepared herself for the jaded darkness that had to come with a man who'd just learned that the evil he'd been fighting all his career was a drop in the bucket compared to the evil that existed in secret. So why was a lump forming in her throat, which was so tight she was scared to breathe?

"Mac wants to meet with you," she said, having practiced this speech to so many hotel mirrors since she began her search that she had it down pat. Mac Mancusi had been the Chief of Detectives when Rick had disappeared. He'd also been the only other Chicago cop to have witnessed the murders that had sent the city into a tizzy. The mayor dead. The lifeless body of one of the most powerful defense attorneys right beside him. Obviously, a murder-suicide. Obviously—only because Regina had manipulated the scene, with Rick's reluctant help, to reflect just that scenario.

In reality, the mayor, a murderous warlock, had tried to kill Mac and Lilith so they couldn't stop him from using the city's criminals to do his bidding, and the attorney, a rogue witch, had been his right-hand man. Mac and Lilith had stopped the evil plot, but at great cost. Particularly to Rick.

"Mac, huh?" he asked coolly. "I figured he was the one who was two steps behind me this whole time."

She eyed him quizzically. "No, that was just me."

"I had no idea you had bloodhounds in your Latina genes," he snarled, emphasizing the Cuban-American accent he'd long ago learned to play down.

She, on the other hand, suppressed the instinct to tell him off in rapid-fire Spanish.

"Our ancestors did find the new world," she snapped back. "What's one rogue cop to a whole continent?" She cursed. Now was not the time for petty exchanges. She did not have a lot of time. "Mac nearly died that night, Rick. Took two months before Lilith recovered completely. If not for them, a lot of people would have fallen under the influence of a very evil man."

"He wasn't a man," Rick corrected, his frown revealing

new lines on his once smooth and youthful face. He'd aged in six months. Physically and spiritually.

"He nearly killed your best friend," she insisted, her heart cracking for the degeneration of the man she'd known, the man she knew he could become again, if only he could see she was here to help.

"Why do you think I left Chicago?"

"To play vigilante?"

His eyes widened at the snap in her tone.

"You think that's what this is?"

"I think covering up the crime cut at your soul," she admitted. "I think the magical world bursting into your ordered, ordinary life set you on a difficult path you don't know how to get off of."

For an instant, she thought she might have hit a nerve. But a split second later, the flash of surprise in his eyes disappeared.

"Go home, Josie. This is no place for a sweet kid like you."

Okay, that crack made her fingers itch. By nature, she was a pacifist. But every woman had her limits. And one was being called a kid by a guy who'd had to take a very cold shower after the last time they were alone together.

"You're kidding, right?" she asked, incredulous. "Who do you think you are, Humphrey Bogart? John Wayne? More like John Wayne Gacy, if you ask me."

"I'm not a killer," he spit.

"According to whose reality? I've seen the bodies, Rick. I've smelled the stench."

"It's not killing when the monsters aren't human."

"I don't give a damn about *them,* you idiot," she said, marching across the room until she stood at the edge of the bed. One glance into his liquid ebony eyes and her anger abated. He wasn't doing a bad thing. Destroying evil was something he should be proud of. But he wasn't proud—

he was desperate. And that desperation was going to get him killed.

Even after all he'd been through, Rick still managed to look gorgeous. His chest, so naturally tan and sculpted, glistened against his towel and the white sheets beneath him. Josie's body stirred, reacting to his as it had before. As if no time had elapsed. As if nothing had changed, when honestly, everything had.

Good Goddess, she ached to launch herself onto him, press her body tight against his, kiss him soundly and erase all the dark ugliness haunting his eyes and the sardonic lines framing his former devil-may-care mouth. This wasn't Rick. Not the Rick she remembered. Not the Rick she'd fallen for so hard. Not the Rick she could have loved, if they'd only had the chance.

Still, his newly hardened edges made her belly flutter. Not to mention the effects of his naked chest and that oh-so-loose, oh-so-easy-to-remove towel. She had to contain a little sigh and fight the impulse to touch him and see how her pale flesh contrasted against his natural darkness, to tangle her fingers in the hair that spiked across his chest, then grew into a narrow line that led to areas she'd once felt pressed tight against her but had never had the chance to take into her hands.

He looked askance, but when he finally allowed his gaze to linger on hers for more than a split second, she saw a shadow of regret flit through his eyes.

After taking a deep breath, she sat down on the bed beside him.

"Tell me what happened. Tell me why you left."

He shook his head. "I can't look back, Josie. And you need to leave. I'm not the same guy you met six months ago."

"Tell me about it."

He cursed.

"No," she said, laying her hand on his, trying to ignore

the way his bare flesh glistened in the dim light. "Really. *Tell* me about it."

He moved to get off the bed, but Josie held his hand so he couldn't escape. He tugged and turned, revealing a gash across his arm. The skin was pink and puffy. Healing, but with jagged edges that told her he hadn't sought the best—if any—medical help.

He chuckled when he spied the horrified look on her face. "Just a scratch."

"That's what the black knight said in *Monty Python and the Holy Grail* when King Arthur chopped his arm off."

Surprisingly, Rick laughed. Not a hearty guffaw by any means, but more than a snigger, which had to mean something. Like he wasn't totally lost.

"I haven't thought about that in—"

"Six months?" she questioned.

"Longer."

He sat back on the bed and Josie couldn't help but notice that the edge where he'd tucked his towel had begun to loosen. Her heartbeat accelerated. The idea of seducing Rick in order to lure him back to Chicago had come to her as naturally as breathing. The possibility of finally confronting the sexual tension that had first drawn them together made her nipples tight and her inner thighs ache. She'd wanted him for so long—the man he was and the man he'd become, even if she wasn't entirely certain yet who that man was.

With shaking hands, Josie slid out of her leather jacket, revealing the snug tank tops beneath.

He eyed her suspiciously.

"What are you doing?"

"I'm hot."

"Then leave," he said, jerking his head toward the door even as his eyes begged her to stay. Or was that her imagination?

Did it matter?

She smiled. "It's hotter outside. Unseasonably hot for New York City in February. Or haven't you left this hotel room lately?"

"I've left," he muttered.

She stretched, lifting her hair off her back, then arching her shoulders so that her breasts curved enticingly. Cheap trick? Oh, yeah. "Really? When? Because in Philadelphia, you didn't even take a hotel room. You slept in that junker you bought from that all-night car dealer."

"You were in Philly?"

She stood and, with one quick flick, undid the top button on her low-slung jeans. She would have kicked off her boots, but she had some serious misgivings about the stained carpet.

"And in Detroit and in Boston," she replied.

She walked closer to the window and hoped that her silhouette against the neon slats of the blinds pushed the right button. They'd been apart for so long and even then, she hadn't known him that well. But if she could just connect with him, get under his skin, she might be able to lure him back to Chicago. To his friends. To his old life. Out of danger from both the supernatural world and his own self-destruction.

Grabbing the hem of her layered tank tops, she lifted them over her head. She was wearing nothing now but a lacy black bra and unfastened jeans with the edges of her panties peeking out from between the teeth of the zipper.

"Don't do this," he said, his voice more pleading than commanding.

She slipped her hands between her jeans and her hips, tugging the fabric down a few inches, making sure he had a good look at the black lace she wore underneath. "Don't do what?"

Though she hardly trusted her normally clumsy self to step forward when her nerves were jangling like wind chimes in a thunderstorm, she made the attempt and succeeded. She was still three feet away from him, but a warring mixture of desire and restraint clouded his eyes. His jaw was set so tight she thought the bone might crack.

"Don't…" Rick whispered, "try and seduce me."

His tone faltered. The words came out half as an admonishment and half as request. And she knew very well which half she was going to listen to.

She licked her lips and closed the rest of the distance between them in three purposeful steps.

"I'm not only going to try, Rick. I'm going to succeed."

4

RICK CLOSED HIS EYES, but Josie, who smelled of musk and sandalwood and had turned on the full force of her inner seductress, was impossible to shut out. And why should he try so hard? Hadn't he spent the past six months dreaming about her, fantasizing about her, casting her as the star in hot, wet dreams that had left him to take sexual matters into his own hands more times than he had since he'd been a teenager?

Why attempt to resist her? With all the darkness in his life, she was a beacon of light. God knows he needed the light. Maybe a kiss, a taste, would satisfy him enough so he could send her away before she got hurt.

He grabbed her by the arms and swung her onto the bed. She squealed in surprise, but he squelched the sound with a hard kiss. Without hesitation, her angel-soft lips opened to him and he thrust his tongue into her mouth, reveling in the sweet flavors of mint and spring water.

Was it enough to cleanse him?

His mind flew back to the first time he'd kissed her in the kitchen of her apartment, where she'd struggled to find matching wineglasses and a bottle of merlot. The space had been tight, and the contraction of his insides had been tighter. He'd wanted her so badly, but he'd resisted. Josie was a mystery to him—a free-spirited woman who contradicted everything in his ordered and ordinary world.

That, at least, hadn't changed.

And neither had the intensity of their kiss. He loved how her tongue sparred with his, how her moans grew louder when he pressed harder against her. Kissed deeper. With each slip of control, his pleasure intensified, as if she'd come here specifically to wash the darkness from his soul.

He pulled away, but she hooked her hands around his neck and drove her fingers tight into his hair.

"Don't," she said.

"I'm trying to stop," he said, his voice thick and raspy from the past twenty-four hours of trying to forget. He'd smoked, drunk, showered, then drunk some more. He'd worked out, using the hotel mattress as a punching bag, working himself into a sweat that had required another shower and another round with the bottle. And still, the memory of the shadow that had tried to invade his body would not recede. How could he let that filth anywhere near Josie?

She shook her head emphatically. "No, I mean…don't stop."

Despite his best efforts, he couldn't resist inhaling deeply, filling himself with her scent. So spicy. So clean. So devoid of the stench of supernatural evil.

"I can't do this, Josie. It's not fair to—"

"I wouldn't have made it this far if I couldn't take care of myself," she insisted, her blue eyes bright with resolve. "I know what I want. I know what *you* want. Take it, Rick. Nothing is stopping you, least of all me."

Her smile, so sweet yet so seductive, injected a joy into his soul he hadn't realized until now he desperately craved. God, he wanted her. Had wanted her. From the first minute she'd stumbled into him at the police station to the charged evening he'd spent in her apartment, he'd fought against the instinct to seduce this woman he barely knew. Unable to resist a second time, he kissed her again, nearly delirious with the clean flavors of her mouth and the sweet silkiness of her tongue. Her pleasured moans goaded him while the lace of her bra chafed against his bare chest, driving him mad with wanting.

Her mouth was soft, but her tongue was demanding. In seconds, they established a wild rhythm that pumped his blood with lust. She tore at his hair, then dragged her nails down his back, raking his flesh and awakening needs he'd suppressed for months. The lamplight in the cheap hotel wasn't the best, but when he finally managed to pull away from Josie, he saw her with surprisingly clear eyes, his vision focused solely on her instead of what might be coming at him from behind.

"You're just as beautiful as I remember," he said, stroking his fingers from her chin to the hollow between her breasts, then lower, lingering at the laced edge of her panties.

This time when she speared her fingers into his hair, the tug was gentle, teasing. Before she spoke, she swallowed thickly, drawing his attention to the necklace she wore around her neck.

Bloodstone. Smart girl. Six months ago, he might have thought himself capable of protecting her with just a badge and a service revolver. Now, he knew differently.

"I was hoping you hadn't forgotten me," she said.

He kissed her longer this time, slower, allowing the enchantment of her pure, feminine need to push the fear and anger that had driven him all these months further away. Just for a few hours. Minutes. Seconds.

"For the life of me," he said, "I can't remember why we waited before."

"Neither can I, but don't wait now."

He did as she commanded, tugging her jeans off her body and allowing his towel to fall to the ground. Against the stiff white sheets he'd lifted from a nearby discount store to replace the ratty rags he'd found covering the lumpy mattress, her skin looked deliciously pink. Her lingerie, while evocative and sensual, hampered her sweet beauty more than it enhanced it. Josie did not belong in black. In every fantasy he'd entertained since the night he left Chicago, she'd worn crisp, clean white or sensuous, calming blue to match her incredibly expressive eyes.

He removed her inky bra, strap by strap, then hook by hook, until her pale breasts were free for him to touch and taste.

He did both, flicking his tongue over her nipples and then watching with keen fascination as the skin swelled and hardened. He flicked again, this time eliciting a tremulous coo from her lips.

Humming his appreciation, he took her right breast fully into his mouth and, with his hand, pleasured the other until she writhed beside him, her thighs tight. He smoothed his palms over her tense flesh until she relaxed and her legs drifted apart to make room for his wandering touch.

Figuring he wanted too much too soon, he lifted his hand, but she grabbed his fingers and guided him toward his original destination—the warm crevice at the base of her thighs. He laved his tongue in tight circles over her nipple as he dipped his fingers beneath her panties. The warm wetness struck him instantly and he couldn't resist slipping his fingers inside her until she bucked in response.

Sliding upward, he kissed a path from her neck to her lips.

"I want you so badly," he said, his sex tight against her thigh.

She grabbed him hard and stroked even harder. "Then... what...are you...waiting for?"

"I don't have—" he started, but her rhythmic massage of his cock knocked his thoughts of protection into a haphazard jangle of words.

"You don't need," she said, her words clipped. "I'm clean and on the Pill. You?"

"Last time I checked, I was fine. It's been a long time since I've been with anyone," he admitted.

She smiled shyly. "Choosy?"

His stomach flipped with unease. "When the only women you're around are hanging out in shit-hole bars and could turn out to be demons in disguise, yeah. You get real picky real fast."

Still clutching his sex, she ran the tip of her finger over the head, dispersing the pictures in his mind of any woman other than her. "If it makes you feel better, I'm all human."

"Honey, I couldn't feel any better than I do right now. Besides, I know what you are, Josie. An angel. One hundred percent angel."

He kissed her deeply, thoroughly, wanting to learn her rhythms but becoming instantly caught up in the pleasure of her tongue against his. When Josie pressed the head of his penis against her sex, the explosion of sensation overrode all rational thought. He concentrated entirely on pressing slowly into her tightness, his ears trained to hear and appreciate every note of her pleasure, which she sang in one amazingly glorious sigh.

She grabbed his buttocks and spread her legs wide. The hunger of her tongue clashing with his pulled him closer and drove him deeper. Wild urges warred against his instinct to be slow and gentle, if for no other reason than to make the sensations last as long as possible. But in seconds, he was pumping hard. She took his thrusts, lifting her knees, tilting her hips until he hit the sweetest spot in her body and her insides tightened and spasmed and she wept.

One more drive and he tumbled after her. Heat flooded through him and into her. She grabbed him even tighter on his ass, pressing him as deep as her body would allow and then kissed him until the tidal wave of sensation ebbed away.

A lifetime later, his brain cleared and, despite the tiny smile tilting Josie's lips, Rick couldn't believe what he'd done. And yet, he couldn't seem to resist when she kissed the tip of his nose and whispered, "Again."

He cleared his throat, covering a snicker. "Excuse me?"

She shifted beneath him. Though he'd softened inside her, he could feel the tiny quiver that told him she could climax again—and soon—if he only made the right moves.

"Not enough," she answered.

He stared at her quizzically. "Didn't you?"

"Come?" she asked, shifting again so that her nipples rasped against his chest. "Oh, yeah. But I've been waiting for you a long time. You didn't think once would be enough, did you? Or am I messing up the whole angel thing you've got going for me?"

For a moment, Rick stared at Josie as if another woman had assumed her form or slipped into her body. But in her fathomless blue eyes, he saw Josie's unmistakable glitter and shine. His body felt lighter, his heart larger, than they had in half a year.

Josie had come looking for him. Josie had found him. Josie had just made love to him with the wild abandon he'd fantasized about for months, and now she wanted more.

"I'm not—" he started, but with a girlish laugh, she pushed him over onto his back.

Grabbing the damp towel from his shower, she proceeded to undo all signs of their previous lovemaking so they, apparently, could try again.

When she was finished, she placed a chaste but charged kiss on his lips. Then his chin. Then in the center of his chest. When she reached his belly button, he felt a stirring in his groin that had him clutching the loose sheets.

"You will be," she promised, swiping her tongue over the tip of his sex. "Trust me, you will be."

THE FLAVOR OF HIS SEX in her mouth was elemental and arousing beyond anything Josie had ever imagined. Musky and hot and with a bite that reminded her of whiskey drunk straight from the bottle, she couldn't resist plying her tongue and teeth and lips until he lengthened and hardened. She caressed his sacs, slipping her fingers far between his legs, knowing she was driving him crazy. And loving every minute.

"Josie," he rasped. "Josie."

She hummed her acknowledgment of her name, loving the sound on his lips, reveling in how she'd zapped his energy or, at the least, changed the course of his energy from the dark aura she'd sensed when she'd first found him into the pure, white-hot need that surrounded him now.

Wrapping her fingers around him, she allowed the full length of his flesh to play against her palms.

"Stop," he commanded.

With a grin, she looked up at him, asking why with her eyes.

He dug his hands into her hair and, though she could tell it wasn't easy, he pulled her up over him.

"Why are you here?" he asked.

His sex was hot and hard against her stomach. She wiggled involuntarily, hissing with pleasure at the feel of him so close, yet not nearly close enough.

"To bring you home," she answered honestly.

"And you thought sleeping with me would convince me to come along quietly?"

She kissed him, trying to ignore the quiver of her aroused clit and how desperately she wanted him to touch it, touch her.

"I'd never want you to come quietly," she replied, the innuendo punctuated by the way she slid on his body. She pressed her pelvis against his, but with a groan, he braced her hips with his hands and pushed her off. But he didn't push her far. He stretched long against her, and dragged his hand lazily up and down her side, pausing to cup her breast until she arched her back.

"I can't go back, Josie. I can't make love to you again if you think—"

She tossed her head from side to side. "I don't want to think, Rick. Do you? Really?"

His reply was a kiss. Long and soft and sensual so that she nearly forgot the other body parts screaming for his attention. His attendance to her lips and mouth and tongue enraptured her so completely she thought she might climax from this alone.

Then he moved to kiss along her chin and down her neck, suckling on the pulse point she was certain was fluttering at a rapid pace.

"I can't believe you found me." His breath was hot against her flesh.

"You weren't easy to find."

"That was on purpose. Not everyone looking for me wants to make love."

"Then I guess I'm special," she replied.

"Good God, yes. But it's also why I have to stop. Why you have to leave."

He flew off the bed, off of her and grabbed a second towel from behind the bathroom door. His absence instantly tore at her and she slid the top sheet over her, though she made no move to get up or get dressed.

"Don't send me away," she said. "I can help you."

"You think I'm the hunter, don't you?"

"You're a cop, Rick. The evidence proves—"

"Evidence can be misread and manipulated," he spit.

"Did you want Mac and Lilith to be tried for the mayor's murder?"

"No, of course not. But that's not the worst thing that happened that night."

Her chest tightened. "What, then?"

He shook his head. "I'm not dragging you into this."

"I'm not delicate, Rick," she said. "I came here willingly. Because I wanted you. And because I want to help you. But those are two entirely different things."

She gasped when he slid onto the ground, kneeling beside the bed. "I can only satisfy one of your needs then. Don't have delusions about the other."

Josie felt a little crack near her heart, but she ignored the pain and focused only on the here and now. Did he think she'd give up only after one roll in the hay? Having him inside her, connected to her in the most intimate way possible, had only strengthened her resolve. She'd do whatever was necessary to get him back. And that certainly included more than making love, which she considered more a gift to herself than to him.

"I don't have any delusions," she replied, taking his hands and pulling him back onto the mattress. "And I'll put my expectations aside if that will make you come inside me again."

She tore away the towel, draped her leg over his hip, then moved so that his sex was once again aimed at the precise spot where she wanted him. Instantly, her body reacted, sending a trickle of moisture to kiss the tip of his hard, curved head.

"That's all you want?" he said, a smile teasing the corners of his mouth.

She laughed and rubbed her breasts against him, igniting a flame in her nipples she knew only he could douse. "Oh, no. That's not all I want at all."

His eyes half-closed, she finally felt the muscles in his shoulders relax. Not much, but enough for her to work with. Enough to give her hope beyond the morning. "Tell me."

"Why don't I show you instead?"

5

WARMTH, CENTERED DIRECTLY between her breasts, woke Josie
with a lazy smile. Was it Rick's breath causing the sweet sensation radiating on her skin? She fluttered her eyes open at
the same time she reached across the bed.

Cold.

Empty.

Gone?

She shot upright. An instant chill sent her scrambling for
the sheet.

"You're awake."

It took a few moments for her to banish the last vestiges
of sleepiness and realize that, while gone from the bed, Rick
hadn't abandoned her. Had she dreamed him leaving?
Sneaking away in the dead of night? Leaving her to plunge
back into search mode, only this time, she wouldn't find him.

"You okay?" he asked.

He was sipping a caffeine drink from a slim aluminum can.

She blinked rapidly to force the moisture from her eyes,
then cleared her throat. "Sorry. I had a bad dream, I guess."

Only she didn't remember a dream. Just running.

Rick turned back to the window. Sunlight, tinged gray
from a convergence of clouds outside, testified to morning.
After plopping two pillows behind her, Josie sat back and
watched him, wondering. From his perspective, she'd gotten

what she'd come for—the night of lovemaking he'd promised her after their first date, which had never come to pass. She knew without asking that he intended to leave her soon, to part company so she could go home to her ordinary life while he continued his quest for…what? Revenge? Justice? She really didn't understand why he'd taken this fight against magical evil so personally. Though afraid that asking might send him running sooner rather than later, she simply had to know.

"Why are you doing this?"

He finished the drink, crushed the can and tossed it into a wastebasket beside the bathroom door, all without moving from his spot by the window.

"Someone has to," he answered.

She frowned. "Someone is. Quite a few someones. You left before anyone had a chance to explain how things work in the magical world."

"Anyone, as in Lilith's sister? The one who manipulated a crime scene?"

Josie swallowed deeply, wishing she had some of the stimulating drink to kick her brain into gear. She was so not a morning person.

"Mac and Lilith are your friends. Did you want them to go to prison, maybe even get the death penalty with such high-profile victims, for doing precisely what you're doing now? Or were you planning to testify for them in court? Tell a judge and jury that witches and warlocks exist and were attempting to take over the city?"

He snorted and turned back to the window, his stare lost between the grimy slats. Josie dragged the sheet around her naked body and scooted to the edge of the bed. "No one would believe the truth and you know it."

"I didn't want to believe it," he admitted.

"Who would?" she asked. "So you left and started, what,

tracking down other supernatural bad guys to make sure the whole thing didn't happen again? How did you learn how to kill a demon anyway? It's not exactly common knowledge and, from what I've been told, they're impervious to mundane methods of execution."

Rick's stare remained frozen out the window, as still and unmoving as his lips.

With a frustrated huff, Josie slipped into the bathroom, hoping a splash of water would clear her fuddled brain. Notwithstanding what had happened last night, she didn't want to alienate Rick. He wouldn't be as easy to track now that he knew she was on his trail.

And besides, she'd miss him. Even before they'd spent all night making love, she'd felt a connection to him she couldn't quite understand. Yes, she felt partially responsible for him. He had, after all, helped in Mac and Lilith's operation to interrogate the defense attorney at her encouragement. But it was more than that. From the time they'd met, Rick had accepted Josie for who she was. He didn't judge her by her chosen religion or by her less-than-legal past—two secrets he'd used his finely honed cop skills to discover even before he'd asked her out. Despite her weird background, he still liked her. He enjoyed her company. He valued her in ways no man ever had before.

Even last night, he'd said she was an angel. Other women might have found the comparison condescending, but Josie couldn't help relishing the idea that she'd been sent to save him. After their one conversation, however, the rest of the night had been spent communicating with their bodies. She'd been no angel, that was for sure. And he hadn't seemed to mind.

She'd just finished borrowing Rick's toothbrush—hey, they'd swapped more than spit the night before—when he knocked on the door.

"Yeah?" she said.

The door opened, but the only thing that came into view was a hand offering her an energy drink. She took it and placed it on the sink.

"It's warm," she mock-complained.

He pushed in a plastic tumbler filled with ice before she'd even finished the brief sentence.

With a grin he couldn't see, she took the cup and said thanks. But before his hand disappeared, she snatched his fingers.

"Don't leave," she asked.

Even from around the door, he managed to caress her face before he left her to her privacy. She knew he wouldn't go. At least, he wouldn't sneak away while she took a shower.

One look at the condition of the tub, however, changed her mind. Instead, she threw a towel on the floor and washed up as best she could from the sink. As she was fiddling with her hair and wondering if the dark circles underneath her eyes made her look like a raccoon, the warm sensation between her breasts started again, precisely where the Valentine's charm was touching her skin.

Was it warning her?

When she went back into the bedroom, Rick was dressed. The sheets had been stripped and folded and her clothes were piled neatly on top. He was no longer by the window, but sitting on his bed, carefully rearranging the innards of the duffel bag he'd kept near the door. She dressed without saying a word, then sat beside him, not surprised to find the bag stuffed with more dark clothes like the jeans and black T-shirt he wore now, as well as various weaponry. A gun. A Taser. Two knives, one she recognized as a ceremonial athame, not unlike the kind she sold at her shop.

"Mac and Lilith did what they had to," he said finally.

"But you didn't have to leave Chicago. Mac joined up with Regina. He's fighting with her, not against her."

He shot her a confused look.

She wasn't sure how much to tell him. She didn't want to encourage him to continue to fight in any way, but he needed to hear the whole truth. She supposed she couldn't complain if he joined her friends to battle the uglies from the underworld. At least he wouldn't be alone.

"In the witching world," she explained, "there are groups. Protection squads, they're called. They're highly trained witches who fight evil. From what Regina told me, the squads have become, well, rare, but she's working to build them back up after decades of complacency."

"That's why they didn't help back in Chicago?"

She shook her head. "Lilith guessed—and she was right— that the defense attorney who killed that snitch of yours was actually a witch. A black witch. Black magic. He was under the control of the warlock who tried to kill Lilith."

"You mean the guy I voted for as mayor?"

Josie nodded. The newly elected mayor had tried to secretly merge his magical world with the mundane, with him as head of all. But Lilith and Mac had stopped the plan dead. Literally.

She turned and faced him straight on. "The mayor wanted to use Lilith to get to Regina, so Lilith never called for help. When she finally wanted to, there weren't any protection squads to come to the rescue. Lilith and Mac improvised and managed to kick warlock ass, but now, they're both working with the squads, training and increasing their number."

"Mac is training and fighting with witches?"

"It's hard, since he's a mundane, but—"

"But it's not impossible," Rick supplied with a humorless chuckle. "I've done my fair share of damage without any magical intervention."

"Mac has Lilith. He's a part of the magical world now. You're not."

"And I don't want to be!"

He spun off the bed, causing his duffel to tumble to the floor. Josie flinched, half-expecting the gun to go off and kill them both. Closing her eyes, she willed her heart to slow down, but all she felt was the increasing heat of the amulet on her chest.

"Then don't," she said finally. "Come back to Chicago with me. You've killed how many supernatural beings?"

His eyes widened, then narrowed with determination. "Not enough. And not the one I'm looking for."

Josie swallowed thickly. She'd known Rick had been trolling the supernatural underworld, hunting for demons and warlocks. She hadn't known he was searching for a particular one. "Whose trail are you on now?"

He ran his hand over his smooth jaw. "You don't want to know."

"No, I don't. But whether or not I want to know isn't a consideration anymore. Ignorance is no longer an option. All that changed for me last year, same as you, when we were dragged into a world we didn't know existed. Frankly, I wish we still didn't know. Life was so much simpler."

"Ignorance is bliss."

She didn't miss the yearning in his voice. Holding out her hand to him, she lured him back to the bed. He slipped his palm in hers but didn't sit. His fingers were stiff, his muscles twitching, as if he was ready to tug away at a second's notice. She pulled him forward and flattened his hand over the amulet.

"It's too late for ignorance," she said, loving how his dark skin looked against her fair flesh, remembering how much pleasure he'd wrought with those fingers just last night. She couldn't help but wonder if she possessed enough feminine power to keep him close, lure him back, save his life. And perhaps, his soul. It was a lot to take on. She was, after all, just a semi-successful Wiccan shopkeeper with a sordid past and a penchant for choosing men who couldn't possibly love her in return.

"It's not too late for you," he said.

"I may not know everything that happened to you, Rick, but I know enough to believe this isn't your fight."

"You're wrong. It's mine more than anyone's. You weren't there. You don't know."

"Don't know what?"

"What it feels like to fight off some sort of dark entity that is trying to take over your body—probably even your soul."

RICK CURSED. He hadn't intended to tell her. By giving her too much information, he was dragging her more deeply into his fucked-up life.

"What do you mean?" she asked, shock evident in the breathiness of her voice.

"Do you know how warlocks are made?"

She had to close her gaping mouth for a moment before she replied. "They're born. The mother is a witch and the father is human, though he has to be particularly nasty to spawn an evil entity like a warlock. Criminal or psychopath. That sort. Warlocks don't receive their powers until late in life."

"So you have read those books in your back room," he said.

"How did you know—"

He cut her off with a hand. "Do you know how they die?"

"They're half human. They die the same way humans do."

"The body does, yes. Like the mayor. But not, necessarily, the spirit. That one Lilith killed was an old soul. An evil one. He died physically that night, but his essence, the blackest shadow I've ever seen, tried to invade my body."

Her eyes were as wide as her open mouth, which she covered with a shaking hand. He hadn't wanted to tell her the truth, but maybe this was best. Maybe he'd frighten her enough to send her running back to Chicago without a backward glance.

"But that's how demons work. The soul of a warlock transfers into the body of a human."

Rick nodded. "A dying human. But I wasn't even wounded and this thing tried to force his way in. I think he wanted youth. Power. A dying body wouldn't give him what he desired. I suspect that the mayor wasn't some random warlock. He was stronger. Older. He knew what he was doing."

"This is not good," she decided.

He nodded again, appreciating the understatement.

"I don't know why he chose me. Maybe just because I was there—or maybe because of some other reason I'd rather not contemplate. But he's still out there and, unfortunately, he's still looking for me."

"What?" She jumped to her feet. "How do you know?"

He glanced down at the arm she was holding so tightly, the arm that had nearly been sliced off when the demons he'd intended to torture for information had turned and swarmed him instead. She stared at the scar for a long moment before realization dawned in her cornflower-blue eyes.

"Oh, Rick."

"I'm not the hunter, Josie. I'm the hunted. So I can't just go back to pretending none of this exists. You on the other hand, need to forget all about me."

"No way," she said instantly. "You need my help more than ever if this thing is after you."

"*¿Estas loca?* What about your life? You want to lose that, too?"

"I know what I'm—"

Josie screamed. Hunched over, she hissed with pain. Rick clasped her shoulder.

"What's wrong?"

"The bloodstone," she answered, digging into her shirt and pulling the amulet out by the chain.

Rick took the necklace from her hand, careful not to allow the stone anywhere near his skin. The drops of red within the green glowed hot. What did it mean? The stone was for protection. Was it warning Josie to get away from him? To stop dissuading him from the road he'd chosen to travel?

Or was it something more?

He yanked the chain from around her neck.

"What are you doing?"

He scooped up his duffel bag and grabbed her hand.

"Getting you out of here," he answered.

"But what about—"

He didn't give her a chance to finish her question. He pulled her from of the hotel room and had just kicked open the stairwell door when his ears burst with sound—first the shatter of glass, then the crack and pop of ignition. A fireball blew their hotel room door off its hinges behind them and the explosion sent them flying.

In his hand, the amulet burned as hot as fire.

With a thud, Josie landed on top of him. He had a few moments of clarity—enough time to see blood trickling from the corner of her mouth—before he was engulfed in blackness.

6

JOSIE FOUGHT THE PAIN arcing through her body and willed her eyes to open. The strong, bitter taste of blood and the pasty dryness of smoke coated the inside of her mouth. She spit and sputtered and, despite the acrid heat, breathed. Instantly, her lungs seized and she couldn't fight when someone lifted her and started carrying her downward.

Down.

Down.

A curse.

A crack.

Fresh air.

She pulled in as much of the clean oxygen as she could when whoever was carrying her put her down. Only after concentrating for several minutes on nothing but breathing and not coughing out her singed lungs did she realize she was out of the building and Rick, similarly charred and panting, was sitting on the ground beside her, his back against hard concrete.

"You…all right?" he asked.

She managed a nod.

"This," he said, his dark eyes watering as he coughed from the smoke, "is why you have to go."

"What…happened?" she asked.

Rick tugged his duffel bag closer, yanked the tie open and

pulled out two weapons, which he stuffed into his jeans. "Explosion."

Josie wiped blood from the side of her face then, realizing she'd sustained only a minor scratch, looked Rick over.

Aside from a cut above his eye and a smoky residue tingeing his café latte skin a dull gray, he looked fine. Very fine. Better than fine. She had to tamp down her every instinct to keep from launching herself into his arms to celebrate the fact that he was still alive. That they were still alive.

"Can you stand?" he asked.

She moved her legs, then nodded.

"Good," he said, grabbing her hand and tugging her to her feet. "I've got to get you out of here."

Before she could protest, Rick had led her halfway down the block. She glanced once over her shoulder and saw the residents of the cheap hotel scattering from the building like bugs. None of them looked anything but frightened and, though a lot of smoke billowed from the second-floor window where she and Rick had made love, the flames hadn't spread. Not yet, anyway.

She jerked out of his grip. "Stop! Just stop for a minute. I need to understand what's happening."

"Someone just tried to kill us. It's that simple. Trust me on this, Josie. You need to get the hell out of here."

Flames shot from the window again. "Looks like hell is where we were." Still, despite a sudden nauseating wave of dizziness that nearly knocked her to her feet, Josie resisted. "We don't even know who…"

Coughing interrupted her thought and weakened her so that Rick could grab her elbow again and propel her farther down the block. He tried a few back doors then, finding one open, led her inside.

The place wasn't empty. It was the back door of a Mexican

restaurant, best she could tell from the overpowering smell of sizzling meat, chilies and cumin that instantly assaulted her. Rick shot out orders in rapid-fire Spanish that Josie didn't have the time to translate, though she distinctly heard the words for "keep" and "return." For now, she concentrated only on breathing and then, on sipping the ice water someone shoved in her hands. The craziness of being not only surrounded, but doted on, by a half-dozen dark-haired men who seemed to take it upon themselves to guard her, caused her not to realize until moments later that Rick had gone.

"¿Dónde está mi amigo?" she asked.

"El dejo," one of the men answered, gesturing toward the door.

She moved to stand, but he clamped her on the shoulder and forced her to sit. Gritting her teeth, she tried to break away, but the minute she slipped by one, another took over, all of them begging her to calm down. Sit. Wait.

Six months ago, Josie might have done just that. But after putting her life on hold to find Rick and then making love to him all night long, she wasn't going to let him disappear when he'd almost been killed.

They'd almost been killed.

Logic told her that Rick had been the target of firebombing, though who had put the bull's-eye on his back was a question she couldn't answer. If a demon had tried to possess him and failed, would he attempt to kill Rick in retaliation? Rick had shown himself in the window. And she remembered hearing the shatter of glass shortly before the explosion. But Rick had made quite a few enemies while on his private mission to rid the world of evil. Any one of them might have taken the opportunity to murder the interfering human who'd already decreased their numbers considerably.

"I have to find Rick!" she shouted impotently.

But this time, her bellow did the trick. She stormed through the parted wall of male chest and hands and plowed straight into the man she wanted.

His lopsided grin infuriated her. "Going somewhere?"

She launched herself into his arms, but while he tilted his head down against her shoulder briefly, he didn't respond otherwise. She stepped back. "Where did you go?"

"To make sure everyone got out of the hotel okay."

"Are you crazy? That explosion was meant for you!"

"You think?"

"This is no time to joke around," she admonished.

He didn't answer right away, giving her a chance to see the deadly seriousness in his eyes. "Why do you think I wanted to make sure no one died because of me?"

Biting her bottom lip, she struggled to form an apology, but he thanked the men in the restaurant and quickly took her arm and led her back into the alley. He'd tugged her half a block again when she finally broke free.

"Where are you taking me now?"

He grabbed her again and propelled her forward. "There's a bus stop around the corner."

"Where are we going?"

"*We* are not—"

"Don't say it, Rick. I'm not leaving you."

"You don't have a choice."

"Wanna bet?"

If there was one thing Josie had had enough of over her lifetime, it was other people making decisions for her. She cared for Rick deeply, but no matter the circumstances, he had to understand that she wasn't about to let him push her around. She effectively removed herself from his grasp and started marching back in the direction of the hotel. Sirens whined in the distance. She had no doubt Rick was drawing her away from the crime scene for a good reason, but if he didn't plan to go with her, she had no interest in retreat.

The minute his hand hit her shoulder, she snatched it, twisted, turned and sent him flying until he lay flat on his back.

She jabbed a finger in his direction. "I'm not helpless!"

He shook his head, grunting as he swiped street grime and gravel off his ass. "I never said you were."

"You don't need to say it. You show it. Everyone does. I can take care of myself. I can also take care of you," she said, with an extra pointed jab. "And it'll do you good not to forget it."

He shoved to his feet, though she could tell the action cost him, painwise. She certainly hadn't planned to attack the man when he'd just survived an explosion, but Rick needed to know here and now just who he was dealing with. Not Josie Vargas, so-called bubbleheaded blond or Josie Vargas, free-thinking Wiccan aromatherapist. Not everything she'd learned from her mother had been worth forgetting. Growing up under the guidance of a woman with no moral compass, Josie had finally learned to steer her own direction. She wasn't about to let Rick change her back into a malleable, directionless twit without a fight.

With a contrite expression on his face, he dusted off the back of his jeans with his hands. "Josie, someone just tried to kill me. That wasn't a random explosion. Someone tossed a pipe bomb through my window."

"A pipe bomb? You're sure?"

"That's what it looked like," he answered.

She gave a curt nod. "I thought it might have been an energy burst."

He chewed on his bottom lip. Clearly, the possibility had occurred to him, too. "Either way, the danger has escalated. I've never been attacked in the relative open during the daylight hours. Someone's obviously willing to risk everything to kill me and they won't care if they kill you or anyone else in the process. They proved that back in Chicago."

Her heart slammed against her chest, making the amulet quiver against her skin. "What are you talking about?"

Rick stepped closer and lowered his head so that an intimate bubble formed around them. Tension rolled off his skin like heat from a flame. Josie suddenly wanted to skitter backward and increase the distance between them, but she forced herself to remain where she was.

"What did the police find out about the break-in at your shop?" he asked.

Josie had to take a minute to process his question. "What?"

"The break-in. What did the police determine?"

"How did you know about that?"

"What did the police find?" he asked again.

"They figured it was vandals. Nothing was missing."

"Nothing?"

Josie racked her brain, instantly clueing in to the fact that Rick's implication shouldn't be ignored. The event had been so long ago and so insignificant compared to her search for him, she'd hardly given the matter much thought. She'd come into the shop one morning to find her storeroom in a mess. The most disturbing aspect had been the fact that her locked cabinet, where she kept her extensive collection of rare books associated with Wiccan history, had been smashed. But nothing, as far as she knew, had been taken. She'd merely called her insurance company, filed a claim, cleaned up and forgotten the entire incident.

"No, nothing."

He nodded, but clearly wasn't satisfied.

"I'm glad you blew it off," he said. "You might have found me sooner if you hadn't."

"What are you talking about?" She waved her hand dismissively. "It was just vandalism. I probably just pissed off a re-ligious zealot or something. I get crap like that all the time once people finally realize what I sell."

"Had you had threats? Recent ones?"

"No," she replied. "Why do you care? It was no big deal."

"It was a big deal, damn it. Zealots and bigots didn't trash your office, Josie. I did."

"You?"

Instinctively, she shrank back from him and Rick grinned. Smart girl, his Josie. Only she wasn't *his* Josie, no matter what had happened between them last night. No matter how much he wanted to cling to the light that seemed to glow from her heart outward—the ultimate contrast to the shadow that had tried to take over his soul—he had to resist. He couldn't afford for her to be anything more than a fantasy woman who had, however briefly, slipped into his world and made his existence both more sustainable and more torturous all at the same time.

"Locks and security systems don't mean much to a former cop."

"You're still a cop," she insisted, though her voice didn't have that same assured quality he'd heard moments ago. "What did you need that you couldn't ask me for?"

"Information," he replied.

"You could have come to—"

"No, I couldn't. I didn't make that mess on my own. I was attacked while I was there. Look—" He glanced at his watch, inching down the alley as his gut screamed for him to cut the chatter and get back to business. The sirens had already stopped wailing. If he didn't get back to the scene soon, he'd have no chance at pinning down which netherworld nasty had tried to take him out. "There's too much to explain."

Unfortunately, the stubborn set of Josie's chin told him she wasn't about to be put off this time.

"Go back to Chicago," he ordered. "I'll contact you there, I promise."

"I'm not the one who just had a pipe bomb thrown at me. You want me to go back to Chicago? Fine. Come with me. Lilith and Mac are there. They can help—"

"No. If I get whacked, there's no great loss to the universe. You, on the other hand…"

"How can you say that?"

"You said it yourself," Rick insisted, trying for a cavalier tone. "I'm a killer now. I'm no better than the ghouls I'm hunting."

"Well, are you better than the ghouls who are hunting you?" She knocked him hard in the arm, connecting with a particularly sore area so that he had to swallow a wince. "This is precisely the reason why I came after you. You have a good soul, Rick. A rare soul. One that clearly had enough power to keep a very strong evil entity out of your body. This world can't afford to lose you before your time."

Rick winced. Her words sounded far too familiar, like the prophecy his great-grandmother had cast upon him before he was old enough to understand the weight of the responsibility. His *bisabuela*'s words had driven nearly every decision he'd made since then—his friends, his career…especially his bachelorhood. How did a man devote himself to a wife and children when his destiny with danger had not yet been fulfilled?

"I'm not any kind of saint," he insisted.

"Aren't you? We come from such different worlds, Rick. Such diverse belief systems. Not just religion, but the way we were raised, you with honor and responsibility, me with crime and lies. And yet the first time we met, you accepted me for who I am."

"That was easy," Rick admitted. Leaving her, on the other

hand, had been the truest form of suffering he'd ever experienced. But he'd had no choice the moment he'd learned that the monsters he'd feared as a child were not only the stuff of nightmares and R-rated movies, but existed in real life. In real time.

"Accepting me was so easy that you walked away without a backward glance?"

Unable to resist, Rick grabbed her with both hands and tugged her close, trying but failing to resist the elemental pull of her perfume, a scent she'd undoubtedly blended herself specifically to drive him wild. The aroma of cinnamon and sandalwood somehow overrode the acrid smell of smoke, causing him to groan with renewed frustration.

"I didn't want to leave you," Rick confessed. "How could you think that?"

"Why wouldn't I? Six months ago, you walked out of my life—out of *your* life—without a backward glance."

"Five months," he corrected.

She rolled her eyes and tugged out of his hold. "The mayor died last August. No one has seen you since that night."

"No one has seen me, but that doesn't mean I was gone."

The confusion on her face made him rethink his decision to tell her the rest of his tale. But maybe if he owned up to his betrayal, Josie would leave. For good.

"I came to find you after it all went down," he began.

"I was at the hospital with Lilith."

He nodded. "I figured as much. So I went to church instead. Old habits."

"Might have saved your life if that thing was still after you."

"It did, or so I discovered the next day. I came to your shop again, but you weren't there."

"By then I was looking for you."

He shrugged. "I couldn't call. The mayor was corrupted. Mac had just conspired with two real witches to cover up a crime, justified or not. I didn't know what the hell was going on. I knew you kept all sorts of magical paraphernalia in your shop, so I broke in. I started looking through your books. I read all night. Once I realized what might be after me, I decided I couldn't contact you. I couldn't bring something so disgusting and dangerous into your life."

She started to speak, but he cut her off with fingers over her lips. Big mistake. An electric sensation slipped through his body, knocking down his determination to run her off. How much more comforting would it be to cling to her light in the face of so many shadows?

He tugged his hand away.

"What is it?"

"Nothing," he said. "My hands are dirty."

She smiled, her blue eyes twinkling so brightly he had to look away. "That's okay. My whole face is dirty. Tell me the rest."

"There's no time. I have to get back—"

She shook her head stubbornly. "Tell me how my store got trashed. Tell me why you led everyone to believe you'd left town the night the mayor died."

Beyond the skyline, he could still see the dark gray billow of smoke. He had a few more minutes at the most. Once his attackers realized that he hadn't died in the explosion, they'd leave, but they'd certainly try again. He needed to turn the tables and take the offensive, but he couldn't do that until he ID'd which supernatural lowlifes had tried to take him out.

He'd make this quick.

"I suspected that the corruption that had reached the city's highest office might have crept into other areas, so I stayed in Chicago. I mean, Mac had been suspended, hadn't he? With no argument from the chief at all."

"You thought the chief was under the mayor's influence?"

"I didn't know."

"Why didn't you contact Mac?"

"In retrospect, I should have," he admitted. "But he was in deep, too."

"But on the good side!"

"Depends on your definition of good, doesn't it?" Rick challenged. "It's one thing to accept that you worship a goddess and that you believe in a power drawn from the natural elements, but it's something else altogether to make things appear and disappear out of nowhere and throw hot balls of fire across a room to kill someone from the inside out."

The images flitted into his consciousness, no matter how hard he'd tried to block them. Rick had seen fire spew from the mayor's fingertips. He'd seen the devil-red glow of hatred in his eyes. He'd watched his friends fight for their lives, too stunned to react, too stunned to understand that his entire life had just been turned upside down. And then he'd been nearly invaded, nearly crushed by a dark entity that hadn't been happy at all when he'd managed to resist.

"Lilith is your friend, too," Josie said, softly. "You never had any trouble accepting her psychic abilities when you were on the force."

"That's not true. I had a lot of trouble. But I was a cop and to stop the bad guys, I was willing to use whatever means necessary. Besides, having some premonitions or keying into someone's thoughts was nothing compared to what Lilith did when the mayor attacked. Regina told me as we were cleaning up. Your best friend had channeled Mac's rage so she could stab a man to death with a knife especially made to kill magical evil."

Josie's shoulders sagged. Only fifteen or twenty minutes had passed since the explosion and escape from his hotel room. The shock had to be wearing off. More than anything, he wanted to get her to safety, but he had no illusions anymore about Josie's determination. She wouldn't go willingly. And time was running out.

"Look, I have a lot you need to know," he said, "but the fire department and cops are likely at the hotel right now, putting out what's left of the fire. I need to get back there."

"Excuse me? Do you want someone to finger you as the guy who was staying in the room that got firebombed?"

"No, but I want to see who's standing in the crowd, watching the aftermath of their handiwork. I won't stay long."

Josie's face tightened as she considered him. "You can't go back again. It's too risky."

"At this point, just breathing is a risk for me. I'm sorry you're caught up in all this, Josie. You should have let me disappear."

She grinned. "I couldn't. I had to know what happened to you. I had to know, even more than that, what might have happened between us if you'd stayed."

Rick swallowed the clump of regret that had formed in the back of his throat. He'd tried not to allow too many what-ifs and if-onlys into his mind. They were worse torture than demons or warlocks could ever dish out. "We'll never know. I had no business letting you into my room last night."

"You didn't exactly let me in," she reminded him. "And you could have resisted my attempt at seduction."

"No," he replied firmly, running his fingers along her chin and tilting her face to the precise angle for a deep and soul-searing kiss. "I couldn't. But I will now."

With an arched eyebrow, she slid her smoky hands into his hair and tugged her body closer until the softness of her curves were flush against him. "You think?"

"I know," he said firmly, though he couldn't quite manage the strength to push her aside. "If I don't resist, you'll die."

"You've got it all wrong," she insisted, locking her arms around his neck. "If you resist, *you* will die. I'm going to help you live, whether you like it or not."

7

"THERE."

Rick leaned around the corner of the building and pointed at the crowd gathered across the street from the hotel. He didn't have to look long to find the demons milling alongside the curious. He could practically smell them from across the street, despite the overwhelming odors of charred drywall and burnt decay blossoming in the billows of smoke still issuing from the old hotel. Since the magical parasites infected the dead bodies of criminals and reprobates, their numbers burgeoned in big cities. Rick guessed the overall population was still relatively small, however, since to make a demon, you needed a dying warlock and a soulless human in close proximity at snuff time. But it only took one to try and kill him and from what he could see, there were two.

Josie peered over his shoulder, her perfume drifting into his consciousness. He couldn't help but inhale deeply and erase the demon stench from his mind.

"The guys in the Mets caps?" she asked.

Rick spun on her, surprised she could pick them out in the crowd. "How'd you know?"

"No one in this neighborhood roots for the Mets."

Took him a second to realize she was joking. He took her hand and together, they wove through the maze of parked cars and fire trucks to the opposite side of the street. Once they were hidden behind a stand selling empanadas and bottled water to the horde of people who'd swarmed the street to watch the excitement of the fire, Rick formulated a plan.

"How'd you really spot them?"

Josie glanced down at the amulet Rick had returned to her once he realized he wasn't getting rid of her anytime soon. "I just looked until it burned."

"Handy little trinket," he commented, grateful that the necklace gave him an excuse to ogle Josie's breasts. They really were perfect. Curves like hers could make a man forget the ugliness in the world. At least temporarily.

Clearly, she understood the power. She arched her back enticingly and scooted closer. "A closer examination might not be a bad idea," she suggested.

His mouth watered, but he swallowed thickly and cleared his throat. "You're torturing me, you know that, right?"

She smiled. "I'd like to think my idea of torture is better than theirs."

"Much better, but your type won't help me find out who sent them to kill me. To kill *us*."

"You try to kill them, they try to kill you. Until one of you succeeds, that's all you have to look forward to."

Rick turned away, but her words lingered. Josie had an eerie way of saying exactly what he knew in his heart but didn't want to say out loud. Self-fulfilling prophecies were scary prospects in his family, particularly after what his great-grandmother had told him all those years ago. She'd claimed he was destined to defeat a great evil. Was this it? And would he have to devote every waking moment of every day to completing his task?

"What?" Josie asked, as if sensing the momentary lapse of introspection.

"Nothing," he insisted. "It's a conversation for another time and place."

Or, perhaps, for ignoring completely since the outcome was not only predictable, but depressing as hell.

The crowd groaned collectively when the paramedics strolled out of the building, empty gurneys signaling that no one needed medical attention. The firefighters had shifted from rescue mode to cleanup and the cops on the scene started to disperse the bystanders. The demons backed into the surge of humanity, their caps barely visible. The time to act was now.

"Wait here," Rick ordered, but wasn't entirely surprised when Josie shot back with a defiant, "As if."

Rick had two choices. He could concentrate on catching up to the demons and learning who'd singled him out for a hit, or he could worry about Josie. He had to admit, if only to himself, that she'd proved quite resourceful so far. She'd found him, for one. For two, she'd managed to get that amulet from the Guardian witch that had warned them of the attack. The split second head start had saved their lives. His choice ended up fairly obvious, didn't it?

Head down but eyes focused forward, Rick pushed through the crowd and rounded the street corner, barely aware of Josie behind him, yet certain she was there. When his prey turned into a dark alleyway that he knew led to a sewer access pipe, he increased his speed. By the time he entered the shadow between the two buildings, he had his modified Taser in one hand and his gun in the other. Without hesitation, he fired a long, blue streak of ramped-up electricity into the head of the demon who'd bent over to remove the sewer cap. The beast dropped, smoking and unconscious.

"Don't move," Rick ordered the second demon, leveling his gun so any bullet fired would enter the monster's skull.

"That won't kill me, human," the demon muttered. So this was an older demon. The tongue had already split down the center, adding sibilance to its saucy tone.

Rick adjusted his aim, fired and took out the demon's kneecap. It howled and dropped to the ground, clutching its wounded limb. Demon blood coagulated quickly and bones reformed at a rapid rate. He knew the pain from the injury wouldn't last, which was why he strode forward confidently and pointed the gun at the demon's groin, prepared to use another shot to make his point. Muscle and skin took longer to regenerate.

"Who sent you?" he asked.

The demon writhed, but his howls had lessened to a pathetic whimper.

Rick fired again, shifting his aim at the last second so that the bullet pinged the ground between the demon's legs and sent a shard of concrete flying at his own cheek. The cut stung, but Rick held steady, only partially aware of Josie's surprised yelp from behind him.

"Tell me who sent you or I'll pump you with holes and leave you. They'll feed on you. Even now, the stink of your blood is in the air. The others will come. They'll eat you alive."

Rick watched the terror sneak into the demon's cloudy eyes and tried not to grieve for the human who'd been taken over by the hellish beast.

"Kill me," the demon begged.

Rick shifted his arms, aiming the modified Taser at the demon's chest as a sign of good faith. Unlike the mayor in Chicago, who was a rare warlock that willingly harbored a demon soul, this creature was pure demon. The only way to dispatch him, therefore, was with concentrated electricity straight to what was left of the human heart—a jolt like the type wielded by powerful Guardian and protectorate witches. In the absence of such magic, he'd created this weapon. Didn't do the job quite as neatly as energy bursts, but beggars couldn't be choosers.

"Tell me who sent you," he ordered.

"You're sticking your nose where it doesn't belong, human."

"Doesn't it?" Rick said, pressing the button on the Taser softly so that the metallic end crackled with deadly blue fire. He bent closer and his eyes watered from the horrible smell. "I'll ask one more time before I turn and walk out of this alley without a backward glance. Who sent you?"

The demon choked, "Ru…hin."

"Ruhin?" Rick repeated.

Josie stepped forward. "What's ruined?"

The demon's eyes widened, his head jerking toward the sewer grate and the clawing noises raking across the metal beneath them. He stared back at Rick with pleading in his eyes and when Rick stood straighter to leave, Josie squeezed his shoulder. Instantly, her clean, sweet scent countered the rising miasma of blood and death and evil emanating from the demon's bloody wounds. He inhaled deeply and the rage that had been thrumming through his bloodstream instantly morphed into hot need.

This was why having a woman along was not a good idea. Especially not a woman like Josie. His hand on his weapon slackened.

The demon's tremulous voice broke into his fantasy. "Finish me."

Rick shrugged away from Josie's touch and fulfilled the creature's request. He then grabbed Josie's hand and tugged her out of the alley just as he heard the sewer cap behind them clang open on the concrete ground.

Josie moved to turn around, but he jerked her back. "Trust me," he said coldly, "you don't want to see."

"There are more of them," she pointed out. "Aren't you going to kill them?"

He clucked his tongue. "When they're feeding, it's like fish in a barrel. Where's the sport?"

Despite his cavalier words, Rick ached to turn around and finish them. He remembering how the images of making love to Josie had distracted him just before he made the kill. In the shadowed dankness of the alley, he'd once again caught sight of a metaphorical beam of light, light he now realized he needed after so much abject darkness. But he couldn't afford to bathe in Josie's glow at this very moment. Not when the price could be her life.

He tucked his weapons into his clothes and squinted against the dull, cloudy gray sunlight above them. He pulled Josie back to the street of the hotel, still peopled with firefighters and the occasional onlooker, then led her to the trashcan where they'd stored his duffel. He lifted the bag out, stuffed the gun inside, but kept the Taser tucked beneath his shirt.

When he turned and finally faced Josie, he was shocked by the look on her face. Instead of fear and loathing, she was tugging and twisting the braid she wore along the side of her pretty face, deep in thought.

"What was he talking about? What was ruined?" she asked, her voice lilting with curiosity.

"Not ruin…*ruhin*. Or *Ruhin*. Capital *R*. I'm not sure if it's a proper name, but it's a Hebrew word which means 'evil spirit.' It's an old word. Very old."

"And that means?"

Rick's mouth suddenly dried. He didn't know everything there was to know about demons, but he'd run across the name Ruhin once and the memory of what he'd read sent a shiver down his spine that cut like ice. "It means this is more trouble than I thought."

"*More* trouble?"

"According to the books in your office, much more," he replied, slinging the duffel over his shoulder, then leaning his head to the left, indicating it was time for them to move faster.

"I guess you don't know what kind of books you have in that locked case of yours."

She frowned. "I bought every single one of those books myself. Just because I haven't read all of them cover to cover doesn't mean I don't know what I have."

"Maybe you should plan for a little more bedtime reading then," he said, but instantly changed his mind. Reading the stories in her collection would ensure she'd never again enjoy another good night's sleep. He knew he hadn't. "Scratch that. Those books should be read in broad daylight."

"We can—as soon as we get back," she said stubbornly.

"Great idea. Why don't you go back and do some research and let me know what you've found out?"

He took her hand when she refused to move forward and started toward the nearest bus stop. A buzz of awareness shot from her hand into his and though his skin ignited yet again, he ignored the lust and pushed them onward. The being after him now, potentially, had a name. Ruhin. An ancient name and, from what he knew of supernatural genealogy, that was never good news.

First things first. He needed to get Josie out of East Harlem. He'd worry about getting her back to Chicago later. As for getting her out from under his skin, he was screwed.

For the first time this morning, Fate smiled—a bus was pulling up to the nearest stop just as they were crossing the street. Rick hadn't been in New York long enough to know where the thing was going, other than out of the area. They sat in silence together, ignoring the strange stares from the other passengers at their dirty, smoky clothes.

"We should change," Josie said as she leaned in to whisper in his ear.

"No time," he replied. "I want to get you out of the city before nightfall."

She groaned. "Rick, just drop it. I'm not leaving, and you can't make me. And if you try and ditch me, I'll just follow your trail. It won't be easy, but I've found you once, and I'll find you again."

She didn't bat an eyelash at his frown, but stared at him with a determination he knew he'd be a fool to fight. If she tried tracking him while demons were still on his trail, she could end up in worse trouble than if he simply kept her with him and tried to avert any danger aimed at her.

"Why are you so hell-bent on helping me?"

She slid her grimy hands around his arm, her fingers compressing at just the spot where his scar began. "Because I care about you. Is that so hard to believe?"

"There's more to it. We barely know each other."

Her smile burned right through the layer of protection he'd been trying to build around his heart. "How can you say that after last night? I know precisely where to press to…"

Despite the crowded bus, or perhaps, because of it, she slipped her hand down the front of his dark jeans without anyone noticing and although she barely touched him, his dick sprang to life as if she'd encircled him with her hand. The promise of what could be once they found a place to hide overrode every other thought in his brain.

"You're cruel," he said.

She quirked an eyebrow. "You think?"

Leaning closer, she swiped her tongue just at the pulse point of his neck, then sat back into the seat. She'd hardly had time to dress this morning and had clearly forgone her bra. Her nipples peaked hard and high through her tank top. He couldn't help but look around to see who else had noticed.

Unfortunately, at least two guys had. Whose chin was about to drop clear to the floor and another whose lecherous smile made gooseflesh pop all over Rick's exposed arms.

He tugged Josie close, leaning around to cover her with his body.

"You're attracting attention," he chastised.

Her eyes glittered with wicked delight. "Am I?"

"And you're trying to distract me."

She licked her lips seductively. "Is it working?"

"Yes, damn it."

"Good, then let's get off this bus and take a cab to where I'm staying," she declared.

"What? You have place here?"

She stood and sniffed disapprovingly at the smiling guy who hadn't taken his salacious stare off of them. Rick grabbed his duffel and squeezed tightly and possessively behind her, not only to make sure the jerk knew that Josie belonged to him, but to hide his burgeoning erection.

As if she'd lived in New York City all her life, Josie confidently jumped off the bus and hailed a cab. They slid into the backseat together while she rattled off an address to the driver.

Twenty minutes later, they didn't stop at a hotel or an apartment complex, but at a shop off the beaten path with a dark front window painted with an enormous eye. Rick instantly recognized the other symbols as decidedly pagan. The Crescent Moon clearly catered to Josie's kind of crowd.

She asked Rick to wait with the cab, but he wasn't about to let her go anywhere alone after all that had happened that morning. He paid the fare and followed her inside. A chime above the door tinkled, and he was instantly hit by the overpowering smells of earth and candle wax.

His duffel knocked into a basket of softly tied bundles, which tumbled to the ground. Ignoring the mess, Josie guided him into a tight aisle, threw her arms around him, pulled him close to her body and kissed him soundly.

Rick's body instantly responded. Blood flooded to his

groin, making his head spin in a delicious dizziness. She tasted of smoke and fire and yet he feasted, exploring every curve and crevice of her mouth with his tongue, imprinting all her flavors into his memory.

She didn't hold back, either. Tearing her fingers through his hair, she pushed against his body, as if attempting to bind him to her in a way that was sexual and raw and elemental. Only after he heard movement in the back of the shop did he muster the strength to pull away.

"Someone's coming," he said.

She grinned saucily. "So soon?"

"I mean," he said, swallowing a chuckle, "we're not alone."

She ground her breasts mercilessly against him. "I'm not averse to an audience."

A tiny, uncertain voice in the back of the shop called, "Hello?"

Josie leaned back but didn't disengage. In fact, she swiveled her hips, milking a tortured groan from his lips as her soft sex bore down on his erection.

"I guess we both need to practice a little patience," she said, then wandered off to buy whatever she needed while Rick stayed in the shadows and tried to will his body to return to normal.

Though nothing was ever normal with Josie around—and he couldn't deny that her brand of unexpected and unusual was the best he'd had in a very long time.

8

JOSIE SPUN around the corner and yelped, surprised by a woman brandishing an extra large cassava root.

"What are you two doing back there? This isn't a hotel," the dark-skinned woman shouted in Dominican-accented Spanish.

"Sorry!" Josie said brightly, her hands outstretched and motioning for the woman to drop her tuberish weapon. "You are open, aren't you?"

The woman's eyes went from wide with anger to narrow with suspicion. Josie brushed her hair back so both the bloodstone necklace and her pentagram earrings were obviously displayed. The shopkeeper's expression softened, but not by much.

Josie decided to pull out a secret weapon and started speaking in Spanish. She was by no means fluent, but she could hold her own. Instantly, the woman smiled and proceeded to help her find all the ingredients she needed. First on the list—more sage, although she supplemented the protection properties with a bundle of angelica root and a bouquet of fresh arnica and bay laurel. Second, she assembled the ingredients of a mind-clearing potion. She wasn't versed in the creation of elixirs like some magical witches, but she knew enough to buy a supply of lavender, moss oak and spearmint. Brewed with just the right amount of concentrated, powdered valerian root and a dash of euphrasia, it would not only help Rick sleep without booze, but also make his rest clearing to the brain.

For good measure, she grabbed some patchouli and sandalwood. For lust.

A perfect combination really. They'd need rest after they worked off the sexual energy that had been spiking through both of them all morning.

Making love last night had taught her what she'd been missing for all these months. And after watching Rick in action, she had to admit she was more turned-on than she'd been her entire life. Josie had always considered herself peaceful and nonviolent, but Rick was right—the creatures who had tried to blow them up were no longer human. No mercy was left in their withered bodies, and Josie had a healthy predisposition for self-preservation. Rick's cool control in the face of such pitiless monsters made her want him even more.

Thankful for the fact that she'd tucked her driver's license and credit card into the pocket of her jeans, she paid for her purchases, keenly aware of Rick's gaze burning the back of her neck when he wasn't staring out the window to make sure they had not been followed. Once she had two handwoven bags full of supplies, she slid one over each shoulder and rejoined Rick at the front of the store.

"What did you buy?" he asked.

"You weren't listening?"

"Yeah, I was listening," he replied, "but I had no idea what you were talking about. Roots. Herbs. Oils."

She nodded. "Not exactly lunch, but we'll pick something up on the way."

"On the way where?"

"You'll see."

Josie had never been happier for her connections with other Wiccans than she was right now as she led Rick to another bus stop down the street, recognizing the route from her explorations of the city while she searched for Rick. He'd divested her of both bags, which he carried in his left hand, keeping his right free to cradle the duffel bag stuffed with guns, knives, Tasers and the like. But they were both packing weapons. Hers were simply of a more subtle variety.

She directed him to exit the second bus about fifteen minutes later on a corner that had grown familiar since Josie had arrived in New York two weeks ago. She waved at Mario, a cab driver who was sitting on the hood of his car, chatting on his cell phone while Iris, his wife, ran the coffee stand outside the building where Josie had been staying. The smell of Iris's freshly baked *pasteles* lured her instantly over and she wasted no time in ordering two large café con leches and a half dozen of the Puerto Rican-style meat pies, as well as a half dozen filled with guava and cream cheese.

"Hungry?" Rick asked over her shoulder.

"Starving," she answered matter-of-factly, not ready—yet—to indulge the sensual rumbling in his voice. "Aren't you?"

"Surviving a war zone tends to heighten the appetite," Mario announced as he strode around the umbrella-topped stand to give them both a keen once-over. "Where've you been?"

Josie tamped down a smile. Mario, who seemed to hang out on the street outside the apartment building more often than he actually drove his cab, had established himself as the fatherly type from the moment they'd met, particularly once he'd figured out which digs she was staying in. Seems he'd been friends with the previous tenant, who'd managed to get herself into a heap of trouble chasing after a man who didn't want to be found. Mario hadn't offered many details, except to assure Josie that in the end, things had worked out. Her instincts told her the cabbie was caring, not creepy, but from the suspicion narrowing Rick's eyes, he didn't yet share her opinion.

She wiped her face with a napkin she'd tugged out of the dispenser on Iris's cart. "You know, this city of yours is just filthy."

Mario sniffed, not buying her excuse for a minute. Instead, his gaze raked over her shoulder and focused on Rick. "Heard there was an explosion in East Harlem."

Josie straightened as Iris, a pretty, brown-eyed woman in her sixties, patted the cabbie on the shoulder indulgently. "Always listening to that scanner. *¿Cómo se dice?* You can take the cop out of the precinct, but you can't take the precinct out of the man? You shouldn't have told him where you were going," she said to Josie.

"Used to be a cop?" Rick asked tightly.

"NYPD," Mario responded, pride puffing his slightly paunchy torso. "Thirty-five years. You?"

Josie held her breath. Somehow, if Rick ponied up to his previous career, he wouldn't seem so lost.

"I'm not from New York," Rick replied.

Mario nodded but let the evasion go. "Hardly anyone is nowadays."

Josie accepted the box of *pasteles* from Iris, balancing the coffees on top and, with a tilt of her chin, pointed Rick toward the steps that led up to the apartment. He swung the duffel across his back and took the snacks from her while she punched in the code that gained them entrance.

"You rented an apartment?" he asked.

"Like I could afford Manhattan rent? No, this place belongs to a friend. She travels all the time and told me I could stay here as long as I needed to."

They fumbled and balanced and shifted bags and boxes until they made it to the third floor without spilling anything, stopping on the second floor landing to inhale two *pasteles* each, neither able to resist the smell any longer. Josie retrieved the spare key from a trusted neighbor, who sized Rick up with bold disapproval. Of course, both of them looked like they'd been to hell and back.

Literally.

But after throwing out a casual comment about an adventure exploring an old, burnt-out building for a potential real estate investment, the neighbor handed over the key and shut his door with a smile, clearly appeased.

"What a cool liar you are, Josie," Rick quoted.

She used the key to the apartment, hefted the coffee and pastries into her arms and shot him a feigned withering look. "Frankly, Rick, I don't give a damn."

His chuckle heartened her, especially against the silence in the minimally decorated two-bedroom apartment. Sparse but cozy, the apartment had given her a little bit of home after months of bland hotel rooms.

"Why don't you use the shower first," she suggested, handing him a coffee. "I'll keep these warm in the oven."

Rick sidled up to her, the hungry look in his eyes having nothing to do with the savory scent of the spiced meat and fruit pies still lingering on their palates. "Come with me."

"Now who's the one trying to use sex to get what he wants?" she asked, placing her hand squarely on his chest to keep him from advancing farther, even though she really wanted to strip him bare.

The power of her attraction to him almost felt magically enhanced, but she knew that wasn't the case. She wanted him desperately, and her soul fed off his touch. He was darker. Tortured. Gruff and tense where he used to be laid back and unflappable. He was no longer the man she'd desired six months ago.

Of course, after all that had happened to her, she wasn't the same woman, either.

Where Rick had been steadfast and reliable before, now he

was a mass of contradictions. Where he'd been a man with strong goals and clear-cut ideals in the past, now he was operating a live-in-the-moment existence where death was just a dark shadow away. With her unconventional childhood and less-than-popular choice to practice Wicca in a world that regarded all pagan religions with deep suspicion, she'd longed for a man to add normality and maybe even a little respectability to her life.

Now, he was haunted by his past and facing an uncertain future.

And yet, she wanted him more than ever.

"I want you, Josie. You wouldn't have slowed me down last night," he reminded her.

"We weren't on the run from certain death last night," she countered.

"I was," he said. "I still am. But you aren't, Josie. You could walk away now—while you still can."

She shook her head, hating him at that instant for forcing the issue when all she wanted to do was make love to him, no matter how she'd tried to slow him down. They'd been so hot and heavy last night. The passion had flown by in a blur. Tonight, she wanted their lovemaking to be slower, more concentrated. She needed to make each and every interaction count if she was going to convince him to return with her to Chicago.

She'd bought all the ingredients to make sure she delayed Rick tonight. Something to protect them. Something to make him sleep. Something to turn him on.

"Look," she insisted, forcing her voice to remain light. "Just make yourself comfortable in the spare bedroom. The shower is really big and—"

He grabbed her by the shoulders. "Don't do this, Josie. Don't try and turn this into some kind of game. That demon.

The name he mentioned. This is serious shit. I won't let you get hurt. I can't."

For a brief instant—so brief, she wondered if she'd imagined it—she saw a flash of fear in his eyes that wasn't entirely for her. He was afraid she'd get hurt, yes, but he was also afraid of something more. Like dealing with the guilt.

She couldn't blame him. He'd already lost his career. His friends. He hadn't spoken to his family in over half a year. Was she pushing too hard by wanting to remain with him now?

The amulet around her neck suddenly warmed. Not a sharp spike in temperature like the jolt that had warned her before the explosion, but a gentle heat that suffused into her skin and seemed to target her heart, breaking down her resistance. Immediately, she dropped the packages and threw herself into his arms.

She forgot the plan. The slow seduction. The need to connect with Rick in a way that might last longer than just one more night, in a way that would justify the love she felt for him—a love that defied all reason. Instead, their clothes dissolved into a pool of charred fabric at their feet. In a haze of desire, Josie managed to direct him into the guest room, where they bypassed the bed and slammed into the shower stall. The cold tile bit at her skin, but Rick instantly warmed her with his mouth on her breasts and his hands everywhere else. When he turned the tap, the initial blast of cold water sizzled off her skin.

The tight space steamed instantly. Josie could no longer think of anything but adoring Rick's body with hers. As an afterthought, she squeezed a puddle of shower gel into a feathery sponge and covered his skin in white, frothy foam. From his neck to his lower back and particularly the full length of his penis, she scrubbed him rhythmically, washing away all signs of their near-death experience, stopping only once after he'd rinsed to drop to her knees, take him in her mouth and suck him to release.

Rick shoved his hands over his face as the water sluiced over him. "Josie," he said, his voice ragged.

She stood, rinsed the sponge and poured another layer of soap onto the fluffy pink bath tool. "You're clean," she said.

His dark eyes penetrated hers with a brutal intensity. He grabbed her roughly and kissed her with a hard desperation that nearly sapped her strength. "Only because of you."

He returned the favor for her, taking his time in making sure he washed, rinsed and explored every inch of her. When he aimed the showerhead at her breasts and then dropped to his knees to slip his tongue into her, she thought she might lose her mind with pleasure.

His loving was intimate and thorough. The sensation of the shards of water pelting her nipples intensified with his every tiny lick. She couldn't resist plucking her own nipples, adding to the crescendo of pleasure singing through her body. He teased her clit mercilessly, toggling her with his tongue, and then dipping deeper until her sweet juices rushed through her like hot lava. She tugged at his cheeks, wanting him to stand, to join with her, to push them both over the edge into sexual ecstasy, but he denied her and made her come with his mouth, lapping up every last spasm.

Seconds later, she realized the water had run cold. And still, they had not made love. Not in the way Josie wanted. Not in the way she needed.

Rick twisted the faucet and leaned out of the shower stall to snag a towel.

"Satisfied?" he asked, blotting the soft terry cloth against her skin as he pressed an intimate kiss on her temple.

She glanced slyly at the beaded water on his shoulder and

couldn't help but swipe her tongue across his skin. "Not even close."

He dropped the towel to waist height, watching as her nipples puckered and tightened anew. "You're cold."

"No," she said. "Just the opposite."

She wrapped her hand around his sex and instantly, he hardened and elongated across her palm. He moved to step away, but instead braced his hands on the tile. "Don't," he begged.

She stroked harder. Faster. "Why not?"

"We can't—"

"We already have."

"You have to go home," he insisted.

"And this is how you're going to convince me? By withholding sex?"

"I couldn't withhold—" He winced when she tightened her fingers around his head and toyed with the sensitized tip. "Don't."

"Don't what? Don't make you crazy with wanting me? Don't remind you how hot and wet I am right now? How tight? How much I want you deep inside of me?"

The necklace still dangling between her breasts grew warm for an instant, then so cool a ripple of gooseflesh prickled her skin. She reacted instinctively, pressing Rick roughly against her, nearly buckling when he surrendered and pushed inside.

"There you go," she said encouragingly, her body primed for the heat she so desperately needed. For the joining she knew she could never live without.

But he held back. Remained stock-still. In the dark depths of his irises, she saw a battle raging. Between release and imprisonment. Between need and desire, which were no longer leading him down the same path. This wasn't just sex to him, which was good, since it wasn't just sex to her, either. She loved him, probably had from the first moment they'd met.

But he didn't think he deserved love. Not after all he'd seen. Not after all he'd done.

"Don't hold back, Rick," she pleaded, knowing she could open his heart again if he'd just give her the chance.

"We shouldn't," he rasped.

And yet, he shifted. He drove deeper. She grabbed his backside and tugged him even closer. He swallowed thickly, but the regret in his eyes intensified.

"What are you afraid of?" she challenged.

"Losing you," he replied.

"Then don't lose me," she said, her eyes welling with tears. Not because she thought he cared for her the same way she cared for him, but because she knew he desperately needed to keep her alive so he didn't have to blame himself for her death. He wore his guilt like a hair shirt, torturing himself into the madness she was trying to rescue him from.

She tightened her arms around his neck and lifted her body full against his. "Don't lose this—"

She couldn't finish her sentence. An intimate explosion parted all words, all thoughts from her brain. Their connection was fast and hard. She was aware of his touch, his kiss, his caress, but her mind mainly focused on the thick, wild pounding of his body into hers. She encouraged him, challenged him, begged him. She filled herself with him until they both came in a cacophony of pleasured cries that echoed against the cold tile and ended when they slid, satiated, to the slippery floor.

They huddled there together, panting and overwhelmed, until Josie grabbed the towel and offered it silently to Rick. He stared at her for a split second, his eyes dark and empty, before he shook his head, pushed the towel toward her and, without a word, left.

Josie started to shiver. Her teeth chattered as she struggled to wrap the towel around her shoulders. It did not help. The iciness she'd seen in his eyes before he'd abandoned her seeped deep into her body, perhaps even as far as her heart.

She'd thought making love to him again would bind him closer to her, but she'd been wrong. He'd found a way to erect a wall between them he hadn't managed to build last night. A battle raged within him that had nothing to do with demons. At least, not the corporeal kind. And, she had to accept, probably had little to do with her, either. This was a war he'd been fighting for months.

She could only wonder, now that he'd seen firsthand how much he could feel for her, how much it would hurt if he lost her, if she'd finally lost him for good.

9

"I DON'T SUPPOSE you want to talk about what just happened?"

Rick closed his eyes, blocking out the view of the New York City skyline he'd been staring at through a small kitchen window, wondering if he should leave now or wait and face the music. And Josie wasn't playing some sweet tune, either. Her voice pinged with sharp anger. And he couldn't blame her.

"Not particularly," he replied honestly.

"Wrong answer."

When he turned, his throat constricted at the sight of her. With her hair loose and halfway dry, her skin scrubbed fresh and flushed from their lovemaking, her lips swollen from the harshness of his kisses, she was breathtaking. Swathed in a fluffy white robe, she made him ache for what they could have had—might have had—if not for a cursed demon and his determination to kill Rick. Or worse—take over his body.

It would have been so simple to love Josie all those months ago. Even after discovering that she was nothing like the women he usually dated or imagined himself marrying someday, he knew they could have made a relationship work. She was color to his black and white. Sky to his earth. Peace to his turmoil.

But now, he didn't have the right to love her. He had no obligation to her except to leave as soon as possible and ensure that she did not follow.

And yet, her blue eyes, swelling with barely checked anger, threatened to drown him in such pure, unhindered emotion that he could hardly hold tight to his convictions. On one hand, he wanted nothing more than to send her far away from him, far away from the dirty evil that had nearly snuffed her life this morning. On the other, he ached to press her soft flesh against his hard, aching body and relieve his pain. Physically. Emotionally. Spiritually.

Logic and common sense warred with the elemental pull he'd experienced the first time he'd met her. He'd surrendered last night and again in the shower, but he knew he had to stop giving in to his weakness. He had no business making love to her when leaving her was the very next thing on his agenda.

"Sit down," he suggested, though from the way she crossed her arms over her chest, she'd interpreted his words as an order she wasn't about to follow.

"Okay, don't sit down," he amended, shoving his own aching body into a chair at the table by the wall. He lifted the lid of the pastry box, took out a guava *pastele,* but his appetite betrayed him. He was hungry. He hadn't eaten a real meal in days. Weeks, even. But what he needed to say to Josie turned his raw stomach into a churning mass of acid. He tossed the pastry back into the box.

"I should have made you leave last night," Rick stated plainly.

She hadn't moved. "Maybe you should have. But you didn't. What does that tell you?"

He chuckled humorlessly. He'd given in so easily. Too easily. He'd known that allowing her to remain in his company for longer than a few minutes would put her life in danger, and yet he'd kept her with him all night.

"Tells me I'm a selfish bastard," he replied.

"Is that why you ran out on your family and friends? Why

you've put your life in danger day in and day out for six months? To fulfill some grandiose need for personal glory?"

He met her gaze. The doubt in her blue irises gave him the confidence to say, "No, of course not."

"Then you're not selfish," she concluded.

"I am when it comes to you."

With his foot, he moved the chair across from his, turning it and gesturing for her to sit down. With a semi-reluctant frown, she swayed for a second, then decisively marched across the room and sat, tucking the lapels of the robe tightly together.

After hijacking the pastry box, she selected a savory meat pie and wolfed down several bites before she spoke again.

"I'm not going anywhere."

"That's fine," he replied, suddenly feeling every ounce of the exhaustion he'd been fighting off for weeks. Months, maybe. Lazily, he glanced around the apartment. It wasn't huge, but it certainly wasn't small by New York standards. Two bedrooms, two bathrooms, a cozy living room and a fully functional kitchen decorated in warm browns and reds with a healthy dose of white to encourage light. He could easily imagine hanging out here a few days, indulging his attraction to Josie and allowing the wounds on his body to heal. "I'll clear out."

He moved to stand, but Josie laid her hand firmly over his. "Don't be stupid, Rick. Sit down and eat."

"I can't put you in any more danger."

"No one knows we're here."

"We could have been followed."

Josie stood up, retrieved the herbs she'd bought at the pagan shop and summarily placed them near and around the front door and windows. She muttered as she worked, repeating, he guessed, some sort of incantation. As a nonmagical witch, the words she uttered amounted to a prayer, and for good measure he added a few of his own. He was fairly certain a bunch of leaves and roots wouldn't keep them safe from a determined supernatural nasty, but they had nothing to lose by trying.

"There," she said, swiping her hands and shoving back into her chair. "Even if they find us, they won't be able to enter without experiencing extreme pain. At least, that's what the woman in the store said."

"You told her about demons?" he asked, incredulous.

She rolled her eyes impatiently. "I said evil spirits. Same difference, right?"

"I have no idea." He'd employed similar precautions at every place he'd stayed since his hunt had begun, but he had no reason to believe the herbs actually worked.

"Well, if demons are meant to attack us here, then they will. No sense worrying about it. I'd rather worry about you. About us."

"There is no us, Josie," Rick said, hating every syllable of every word. "There can't be."

Josie stared at him for a long moment, her eyes narrow and intense. He thought she might argue with him again, but instead, she tilted her chin at him defiantly and went back to the bags on the counter to finish unloading her purchases. "At least wait until night before you run out on me. You'll need the cover of darkness."

He eyed her suspiciously. "And you won't follow?"

"I didn't say that," she replied with a sharp grin.

"Josie," he started, ready to protest, but she quelled his words with a weary sigh. She was exhausted. So was he. The best thing they could do was finish off their paltry but filling meal and spend the rest of the afternoon in bed.

Sleeping.

With a snort, he sat back down and polished off two more *pasteles*.

Josie poured them both tall glasses of ice water garnished with fresh slices of lemon, but she didn't speak to him. She set a kettle on the stove and busied herself with picking through the herbs, roots and oils she'd bought at the store, examining and separating them, plucking flowers, measuring with droppers, chopping and stirring stuff into the boiling water until the whole apartment filled with scents that were at once sweet, spicy, earthy and exotic.

As she worked, she hummed, her blond hair nearly completely dry, the edges near her face curling in the steam from the thick ceramic bowl she'd chosen for mixing. Soon, Rick could barely keep his eyes open much less muster the energy to ask what she was doing.

Little by little, his eyelids dropped. He strained through forced slits to watch the way her hips rocked and her shoulders undulated to the music playing in her mind, but eventually he fell asleep.

When he awoke, the kitchen was dark. The aromas from Josie's brew still permeated the air. Once his eyes adjusted to the dim light spilling in from the window, he realized that she'd set a thick, ceramic mug in front of him that still steamed with fragrance. He picked it up, took a sniff and the moment his vision blurred, he pushed the cup away.

"What is all this?"

He heard a soft murmur from the other side of the room. Sleepy and feminine, like a sigh in a dream. He stood, groaned at the aches in his joints and muscles, then stretched and made his way to the couch.

Josie's outline was a sensuous *S* of slumber. Judging by the heat from his mug, she'd just fallen asleep. Still clad in the fluffy robe, she'd drawn her hands beneath her cheek and her left knee was nearly touching her chest. Even in the uncertain light, he could see the contrast of her skin against the white robe and the dark red couch. He wanted to see more of her. So much more.

But he did not have the right.

He couldn't keep insisting that she had to leave him alone and yet continue to surrender to the attraction driving him, even now, to wonder about the flavors of her skin.

He forced his gaze to the window and from there, to the neon-blue clock on the VCR. It was nearly midnight. He had to leave.

Again, she stirred, murmuring innocently, then mumbling something that almost, just almost, sounded like his name.

He took a step toward the bedroom where he'd left his shirt and shoes. He couldn't believe he'd fallen asleep for so long. Sure, his body had been screaming for rest for weeks, but exhaustion alone wouldn't have caused him to ignore every instinct in his body to remain alert, if only for Josie's sake.

And yet, for the first time in months, he'd slept without dreams. No opaque shadows pressed down on him. No flying balls of fire scorched his skin. No glinting knives slashed toward his heart, causing him to spin and take the cut along the length of his arm.

Just sleep. Sweet, invigorating sleep, like what trapped Josie right now. Or else, if she dreamed, her subconscious gave her something more pleasant to experience, judging by the slight curve of her generous lips.

He leaned forward to shake Josie awake, but his hand stayed just inches from her shoulder. She'd shifted into a beam of street light from the window, catching the glow like some sort of otherworldy being. Not the kind he was chasing, but the kind he'd been taught since childhood would intercede on his behalf.

He could spare another few minutes with her, couldn't he?

On the table in front of the couch, he found a collection of unlit candles. With the long matches lying in a decorative dish, he lit them, then turned to Josie, holding his breath.

The flickering radiance created an irresistible atmosphere, just as he'd suspected. Perhaps, as he'd intended. Her lips, so pink and moist, were slightly parted and maddeningly enticing. The lapel of the robe had fallen aside, giving him an unhampered view of her breasts. He dropped to his knees, glanced once more at her sleeping face, then surrendered to sweet temptation.

Her nipple was soft and warm beneath his tongue at first, her skin sweet to the taste. Buoying her flesh in his hand, he suckled her softly, careful not to pluck or prick, but to arouse her as she slept. Soon, she cooed but did not wake. He loved her other breast with equal care, the bud tightening between his lips.

He glanced at her face. Her lids danced with the dreams playing through her mind as he pleasured her. He wished he could look into her mind and see what fantasy kept her in slumber, but the physical lure of her drew him back to her body. Out of the corner of his eye, he caught sight of the necklace nestled in the hollow of her throat. Had it just flared with warm, scarlet light or had it been a trick of the candles in the haze of his need?

God, how he wanted her. Desire surged through him, working out every kink and sore muscle. He realized then that his need for Josie transcended mere sexual attraction. She was a balm for him. A salve. She smelled of natural oils and herbs, scents he associated with the reverence and spiritual healing. She looked like an angel. The symbolism should have sent him running, but on his knees, he could do nothing more than worship her.

He untied the knot on her robe and ran his fingers lovingly along the bare flesh of her waist, stomach and thighs. He lit another candle, then another, lining the tapers along the table behind the couch until her body was bathed in a golden glow. The curls at the apex of her thighs, pale, but dense, shimmered from the firelight. He kissed a soft path from her navel to her sex, allowing her flavors to sit on his tongue before he took a second taste.

Exercising every ounce of willpower, he kept his tongue lax and lazy. He wanted his mouth to be a whisper against her sensitive flesh, a promise of delights that would not yank her from her dream-filled sleep. After a long minute, her clit finally swelled to a delicious point he could not help but suckle. By now, her sleepy moans had increased, though her eyes remained closed. Her hands had drifted to her breasts, her fingers mimicking the soft brush of his mouth over her nipples.

He stripped off his shorts and then gently kissed her face. First above her eyelids, then on each cheek and finally on her mouth. When her tongue twined with his and her hands slid into his hair possessively, he laid his body across hers.

"Rick," she breathed, shifting her hips instantly so that his penis pressed against her. "I thought I was dreaming."

"You are," he reassured, then plunged inside.

Her hot flesh surrounded him and he responded with slow, rhythmic thrusts. He lifted off her high enough to watch as his sex disappeared inside hers, then reappeared, every nerve ending rejoicing in the slick, snug joining. He slid his hand down her thigh, hooked his fingers beneath her knee and lifted so that he could drive deeper and longer, even as he struggled to keep his tempo slow and steady.

Her orgasm started the minute he looked into her sleep-fogged eyes. He gave her one quick kiss, but the moment she bucked and tried to increase their speed, he pulled back.

"No," he said. "Nice and slow. I want to feel every inch of you. I want to burn you into me. You're light, Josie. Light to my darkness. I need you."

She didn't speak. She closed her eyes and bit her lip, but he swiped his tongue across her mouth.

"Look at me," he said with a growl. His cock had hardened to the sweetest pain he'd ever felt. His balls were thick and heavy. But he had to hold back, just a little longer, to bring her the pleasure she deserved. The pleasure he prayed would make her remember him forever, no matter what happened next.

Was it pride? Selfishness? He didn't care.

Because he wouldn't forget her. If he hadn't before they'd made love, he doubted now that he ever would.

She stared directly at him as he watched her climax building in her darkening pupils.

"Oh, Rick. Oh—"

"Shh," he said, grinning. "I could stay inside you forever. Stroking you, feeling those sweet spasms."

She'd begun to pant. He buried himself deeply inside her, then stilled.

"Don't," she begged.

"Let's take a little rest. I don't want you to come yet. When you do, it'll be all over."

"No," she insisted, though he wasn't sure if she was contradicting him or agreeing with him.

Her body trembled, inside and out. Holding himself back caused a similar shaking as the sensation of her hot flesh cradling his erection nearly drove him to madness. He could not draw out the climax much longer. They might both lose their minds.

With her fingers spiked through his hair, she only had to shift her hands to bring his stare back to hers.

"Even when you come inside me, it won't be over. I swear. I—"

But her words cut off. Spurred by her resolve, he'd driven into her hard and deep and fast. In seconds, she screamed out his name, begging him for more, and more he gave her. She wrapped her legs tight around his waist and met his thrusts until he exploded in a final drive that toppled them both over a precarious, exhilarating edge.

THE MINUTE HIS BODY relaxed over hers, his head curled against her shoulder and his hot breath blasting against her skin, Josie grinned. The brew she'd concocted had done its job. Before waking her in what she decided was the most wonderful way possible, he'd finally slept. Yes, he'd been in a chair, leaning against the wall, but he'd slept without stirring. She'd watched him for hours, refilling the mug in front of him, ensuring that the aromatic steam from the potion trapped him in a dreamless sleep.

She had also hoped that a few of the ingredients would do their magic on his libido, so that when he woke, she'd have an easy and enjoyable way to keep him at the apartment for one more night. She hadn't meant to fall asleep herself, but she was very glad she had. The dreams she'd enjoyed prior to Rick kissing her awake had been heavenly and erotic at the same time. She could only imagine precisely what he'd done to inspire such luscious imaginings.

When he moved to stand, Josie couldn't help holding him tighter.

He brushed his lips across her cheek. "Don't worry. I'll be back."

With a pouty frown, she released him. She took advantage of his momentary disappearance into the guest room to dash into the other bathroom and put herself back together. She liked the robe, but her skin was now a bit too hot for the thick terry cloth. She switched it for a plain but filmy nightgown she'd brought with her from Chicago.

Once back in the living room, she moved to flick the lights on, but Rick stopped her.

He was sitting on the couch dressed in boxer shorts and

nothing else, staring at the candles now lining the coffee table in front of him.

"I like the dark."

She arched a brow. "So I gathered."

Her sarcasm won her a rare but devastating smile. He held out his hand to her, which she immediately gave him. He led her not onto the couch beside him, but onto his lap.

"What exactly did you put in that tea?" he asked.

"It's not tea." Her heart skipped a beat. "You didn't drink it, did you?"

"Why?" he asked. "What will happen to me if I did?"

She pursed her lips. "Possibly some hallucinations. Definitely a stomachache, but nothing serious. I knew I shouldn't have used a mug."

Rick laughed. Not a chuckle or a snicker, but a real, belly-shaking laugh that made her entire body quiver. "What's so funny?"

"You, Josie Vargas. You're unlike any woman I've ever met."

"I know," she quipped. "I'm a very heavy sleeper."

His eyes darkened to the point where she couldn't see even a sliver of brown. "I couldn't resist you. Was that the potion, or was that just you?"

"Maybe a little bit of both," she admitted, smoothing her finger around his ear and then leaning down to suck on his lobe. When she spoke, she whispered. "I don't want you to leave, Rick. I don't want you to put yourself in danger anymore. If this demon is after you, don't make it easy for him to get you. Stop putting yourself in his way."

"I'm not putting myself in his way. I'm trying to get to him before he gets to me. What do you expect me to do—hide?"

"If you have to," she replied, entirely serious. "Yes. Stay with me. I'm infinitely more interesting and enjoyable to be around, I swear."

She expected him to push her away, but instead, he slid his hand between her legs, mercifully curving his fingers around her knees. "You're torturing me. I could stay here and make love to you for days on end."

"Mmm," she hummed, lowering her mouth to use tongue and teeth against the sinews of his neck. "Is that a promise?"

The tension in his neck returned, so she suckled harder until his muscles yielded beneath her lips. She didn't want to have this conversation tonight. Maybe when it was daylight and she could convince him yet again that it would be better if he waited until nighttime to move, though she suspected he wouldn't fall for the same ruse twice.

"Josie, this demon isn't going to stop chasing me down just because I hide."

She knew he was right. He hadn't been out hunting this morning when the pipe bomb had been lobbed into their window. She gasped, suddenly realizing something.

"What?" he asked.

She pressed her lips tightly together, not sure she wanted to share this supposition with Rick. But if she wanted him to be entirely honest with her, she'd have to do the same.

"I've been wondering why the demons attacked you in such a conventional way this morning."

He shook his head. "I'm not—"

"What if he was trying not to kill you, but to weaken you? That bomb was loud and did some damage, but it must not have been very strong or the whole hotel would have come down. That place was a tinderbox."

Rick's eyes widened. "You're right. He must have been nearby, just waiting to take me over the minute he—"

Josie tugged him closer, clutching him with such desperation she heard him gasp. But after a long moment, he held her with equal intensity. Couldn't he see how they needed each other? Couldn't he see that there was no way on this earth she was going to leave him to face this battle alone?

"I know what I'm getting myself into," she assured him.

"This is pointless," he said. "We can't keep having the same argument. This demon wants me. It's personal." He slid her off his lap to the couch and shoved both hands through his dark hair. "If I don't find him, then he'll find me. And when he does, you can't get caught in the crossfire. Josie, I couldn't live with myself if you got hurt because of me."

She ran her finger along his forehead, trying to unknit the tightening in his brow. "You don't have to do this alone."

"What other choice do I have?" he asked. "You don't understand."

She could see a battle raging within him, a battle based on information she did not have. Part of him clearly wanted to confess. His teeth were grinding together as if he needed the friction to keep the words contained. But another part of him—the decidedly male, inherently Latino, macho, stubborn part—resisted.

"Rick, what aren't you telling me?"

The necklace around her neck buzzed with warmth.

"Nothing."

"Liar."

"I'd rather be a liar than a manipulative witch," he said, charging to the table and lifting the mug so that the contents sloshed all over his hand.

She laughed. "Insulting me isn't going to make me back off," she sang, levity in her voice. This didn't need to degenerate into a fight. Not after all they'd been through. Not after all they'd shared. The sex might have been just a physical release to Rick, but she'd bet her shop and all the contents in it otherwise. They'd connected. "Fine. Don't tell me your big secret. But you need help and if you won't take it from Regina or Mac or Lilith, who's left? Me."

"Fine."

"Good. Fine," she snapped, then realized she wasn't sure what he meant. "Fine, what? Are you coming home with me, or am I helping you with this demon guy?"

"Neither. I've changed my mind about letting your friends get involved. Call Regina. Call her now. And after I talk to her, you're getting the hell out of here. For good."

10

JOSIE FELT HER JAW go slack. This was not the response she had been expecting. When she finally managed to close her gaping mouth, she narrowed her eyes and stared at Rick's stubborn face, looking for any sign that he was calling her bluff.

He wasn't.

"You don't even know who or what this Ruhin is," she countered, trying to maneuver within the corner he'd backed her into. Yes, she wanted Regina and her protection squads of highly trained witches to take over Rick's self-imposed mission to destroy the demons who had tried to kill him, but she didn't want Regina alerted to Rick's change of heart until she'd convinced him to come home to Chicago and resume his normal life. If he planned to simply keep on fighting alongside Regina—and without Josie—well that simply did not work for her.

She hadn't come all this way, shared so much with him, to let him go now because of some inflated need he had to protect her. Besides, scenarios of a confrontation between a stubborn, single-minded and dangerous Rick and the equally unmovable and fierce Guardian witch played in her mind… and none of them ended happily. Once Regina found out where he was, she could easily send him far away in the blink of an eye. Even if she sent Josie, too, Rick would never forgive her.

He crossed his arms tightly over his chest, wincing a bit at a pain she guessed remained in his shoulder. "I know he's formidable. I know his reputation precedes him if the creature we caught this morning was afraid to say his name. Call her. And then you can go home."

Emptiness swelled around her heart. She couldn't do this. She couldn't leave him to face this battle alone. Not because of any sense of responsibility or out of sexual attraction. Or even Lilith's vision. No, she wanted to help him because she cared. Deeply. In a way she never had for any man before— possibly, for any person. She could not leave him to fend off magical forces on his own, not when she knew that doing so could result in his death.

"You don't want me to call her," she replied.

"Why not? Isn't that why you're wearing that necklace? She gave it to you. You can probably use it to call her. Try."

Josie's hand shot immediately to the amulet, but she scowled all the same. "This isn't a communication device. It's for protection."

His eyes narrowed. "It's Lilith who is your friend, Josie. Not Regina. Not that I got to know her all that well, but my impression was that she's much shrewder than you might think. If that thing was only for protection, it would be doing a better job."

"It saved our lives this morning," she countered.

"Yeah, but it's allowing me near you now, isn't it? A magical amulet worth its salt would put some sort of shield between us, keep me from touching you, keep me from wanting you."

She stepped forward and locked her hands around his forearms. "I'm not afraid of what we've started."

"You should be," he said, his voice barely a whisper. "I'm a marked man."

"All the more reason to open up to me. To let me in. To let me help. Because I will work beside you. Regina won't. As a sacred witch, she's sworn to protect all mundanes from magical evil. She'll take you out of this fight in a split second. I had to convince her to give me some time to try and stop you myself."

"She didn't know about this Ruhin demon."

"No, but she knows that your battles have risked exposure of her world. She can't allow it. I'm surprised the pipe bomb didn't cause her to renege on her deal with me, but she probably couldn't find us. Her magic doesn't allow her to locate mundanes who don't want to be found and clearly, this amulet isn't some sort of tracking device or she'd already be here."

Rick yanked out of her hands and stalked back and forth across the room, dragging his fingers through his hair so roughly, she winced. "I can't let her take over this fight. It's my battle. My responsibility to figure out what it is about me this Ruhin wants so desperately."

As much as it broke her heart to agree with him, Josie couldn't help herself. "I know."

"Then what am I supposed to do? I can't go back to Chicago and pretend none of this happened. I can't fight as long as I'm worried about you getting caught in the crossfire and now I can't call in your powerful friend, because she could banish me to someplace she decides is safe so she can fight my battle for me. What choice is left?"

Josie grabbed his arm, stopping his marching tirade. Her whole body ached for the position he was in, but while he was a mass of conflict and contradictions, she had a very clear idea of what needed to be done. He simply had to agree. "Stop worrying about me. I'm not some sort of delicate girl who can't take care of herself. I've gotten that my whole life, Rick.

And I hate it. I'm smart. I'm quick on my feet. I know you deserve the chance to challenge this demon on your own terms. I respect that now. Can't you respect my need to help you? To be with you?"

His hand clamped over hers. His touch shook with emotion, though she couldn't tell which. Anger? Fear? Love?

Good goddess, let it be love.

"Why would you want to put yourself in the line of fire? You hardly know me. We had what, one date, before I took off?"

"We've had more than that since then."

"You mean the sex?"

His voice brimmed with callous disregard and Josie's chest grew hot as the stone around her neck flared with the same fire as her anger. She stared at him, disbelieving, watching him wait for her inevitable reaction.

Only she didn't give it to him. Maybe that was what he wanted. To piss her off so that she would leave.

Instead, she released the necklace, tucked her hands into the pockets of her nightgown so that the neckline plunged a few inches and smiled.

"That's precisely what I mean."

Soft and husky, her tone elicited exactly the response she'd expected. The hardened expression on his face disappeared and his eyes betrayed his desire. He wanted her again. If she stripped for him now, dropped to her knees and took his cock into her mouth like she desperately wanted to, she'd have him begging for her to stay. But for how long?

"It was just sex," he claimed, though his voice quaked.

"Really?" she challenged, disbelieving. He might be a good cop and a formidable demon hunter, but with her, he was a terrible liar.

"Josie, don't make me do this."

"What? Make you try and convince me that all we've

shared in the past twenty-four hours was lust? Look, you may have fucked me that first night, but you didn't earlier today and you certainly didn't tonight. We made love. You know it and I know it and you won't convince me otherwise. If your plan is to insult me and degrade me so that I'll leave, forget it. I happen to know the truth."

"You don't know anything."

"Then tell me, Rick. Tell me why the demon has targeted you. I think you know. The first time he attacked you, in Chicago, I understand. You were there. Young and virile and perfect to invade. But you resisted. Why didn't he just move on?"

"Maybe because I went after him," Rick admitted.

"Only after you were attacked in my shop," she reminded him. "He struck first randomly, but the second time was deliberate."

He nodded. "I was researching what happened. Digging into phenomena that made his existence possible."

"You were a threat. So maybe that attack was just to shut you down."

"But how did he know?"

Josie pressed her lips together, trying to think of some explanation that wasn't too terrifying to contemplate. "He was watching you?"

"Why? There's only one explanation, Josie, and it's the one that sent me all over the Eastern Seaboard trying to find that supernatural son of a bitch. He still wants me. That's why I attacked first."

"But why *you?* If he's this formidable supernatural soul looking for a body, there has to be someone else that's easier to kill."

Rick smiled humorlessly, then dropped onto the couch, his elbows on his knees and his head in his hands. Josie took a step toward him, then changed her mind, sensing he needed a minute to collect his thoughts. Because she wasn't going to let him weasel out of spilling the entire story this time.

To be on the safe side, she dumped the relaxation potion out of the mug and the pot on the stove, then opened the refrigerator to seek out the bottle of wine she'd put in there the first night she'd crashed at her friend's apartment. Nothing fancy…a cheap Lambrusco, but she doubted Rick would be choosy. She grabbed two glasses, switched on a lamp by the couch to dispel the romantic mood and plopped down beside him.

At the sight of the wine, he groaned in appreciation, twisted off the top and poured until they both had more than enough spirits to drown themselves while he told his story. He took a long sip before beginning.

"Do you believe in Lilith's power of premonition?" he asked, glancing at her from the corner of his eye, not facing her directly.

"You know I do. She's seen the future bunches of times."

"How far into the future?"

She shrugged. "At least six months. She saw me helping you."

Rick nearly choked on his wine.

"Why the surprise?"

He swallowed painfully. "It's not surprise. Just…irony. A vision sent you after me?"

"I was already trying to track you down when Lilith came to me. But I was about to give up. The vision kept me going. Strengthened my resolve."

"Yeah, they do that."

"Lilith had a vision of you?"

"Oh, no. That would have been freaky enough, but at least if she'd told me something about my future, I would have been old enough to take it with a grain of salt. My first experience with clairvoyance happened a long time ago. When I was six."

Josie listened, rapt by the soft tone Rick took when he spoke of his first and only trip to meet his family in Cuba and his remarkable meeting with his great-grandmother. The old woman might have had good intentions, but burdening a six-year-old child with a prophecy about defeating a great evil had been too much.

"You believed her?" Josie said.

"I was six. And to be honest, she scared the crap out of me from the first moment she touched me. I didn't have the ability to explain it then, but now I know that I saw her power. I had no choice to believe her."

"And you think Ruhin knows this about you? That he's the great evil you're destined to defeat?"

Rick's gaze met hers, intense and powerful with a determination that set him apart from anyone she'd ever met. He readily admitted to fear, but he did not allow the emotion to waylay him. His strength under unbelievable circumstances stole her breath. And her heart. Oh, yeah. Her heart didn't stand a chance.

All her life, she'd wanted nothing more than a man to make her life stable, to steady the rocky wildness of her childhood and give balance to the life she'd chosen, a life so often marked by whimsy and unconventional needs and desires.

Only what she wanted now wasn't unique or special or particularly quirky or capricious. What she needed from Rick was the most basic, most elemental desire a woman could have with a man.

She wanted him.

But when she opened her mouth to say so, he cut her off.

"So now you know why I have to take this to the end. I'm destined for this."

"I guess I should remind you that premonitions aren't always right and that what people like your great-grandmother and Lilith see is only one probable outcome."

"You guess?"

"It's the logical thing to say," she assured him.

"When have you ever been logical?" he said with a snicker.

She slapped him playfully on the arm. "Well, yes, that's my point. I should say it, but I won't. Prophetic visions aside, you're engaged in this fight now. You can't change that, I understand. Honest to the goddess, Rick, I understand."

The air crackled between them. Rick slid his hand over her knee and then twined his fingers with hers. His touch was both reassuring and heart wrenching. For the first time since their reunion, his flesh on hers wasn't about sex or seduction or protection. The sensation of his body and hers interacting was simply because they understood each other and wanted the same thing.

"Those creatures in the alley were soulless killers, and they're just bottom tier. This Ruhin is clearly upper echelon. Can you imagine what our chances are of defeating him without serious collateral damage?"

"I'd rather not imagine, thanks," she said dismissively.

"Then you're not ready to be my sidekick."

"Listen, just because I don't want to do something doesn't mean I won't. And here I thought you were starting to understand me."

"I am," he insisted. "As much as any man can understand any woman."

She snickered. "That doesn't say much."

"Well, it's all we've got, that and two premonitions that we're destined to work on this pesky project together."

"Well, I'm going to have to defer to you. I have no special powers except my knowledge of flowers and herbs and scents."

Rick's mouth quirked into a quick grin as his eyes darted to the table where she'd left the potent brew, then back to the couch where, less than an hour ago, they'd made love.

"Those skills are damned impressive."

She didn't try to hide her pride. "Thank you. But you know, that's not all I can bring to the table. I did read a lot of those books in my office, especially after you left. And a whole cache of them that Lilith loaned me. And I'm very good at finding people, as evidenced by the fact that I found you. And at the end of the day, after you've done whatever you need to do, won't it feel better to be with me than alone in some crappy hotel room?"

"Not if it means you get killed."

She toyed with the amulet. "We have a warning system. We have our instincts. We'll have each other's backs."

Rick had always suspected that Josie had a stubborn streak, but he'd hoped, up until now, that she'd been acting on adrenaline and emotion and could be dissuaded once the going got tough. He couldn't delude himself any longer. She wasn't leaving his side. She wasn't meant to.

"Okay, then it's time we did a little more research."

"On Ruhin, now that we have his name?"

"Yeah," he replied.

"I have a laptop in the other room," she said with a grin.

She shot off the couch with a squeal of excitement like a kid who'd just won free tickets to Disney World. They'd both have to be at the top of their game to do this right without either of them getting hurt, so he hurried into the guest room, where he'd tossed his duffel, pulled out spare clothes, checked and double-checked his weapons and prayed that when he went back into the living room, he'd stop thinking about Josie as a lover and start thinking of her strictly as a partner.

He doused himself under a very cold shower before drying off, dressing and joining her in the living room.

Unfortunately, she wasn't going to make his resistance easy. Though she, too, had changed into regular clothes. The cropped, low-slung yoga pants and snug, T-backed tank top that hugged her breasts as if designed to torture him, threw his libido to the forefront of his mind. His dick tugged at the denim of his jeans, but he shifted the mutinous muscle out of his way and charged toward Josie and the computer.

He stopped dead when he was within two feet of her. The alluring scent of sandalwood burned from a candle. Warm and erotic, the fragrance immediately undid all the calming effects of his hasty, frigid shower.

He cleared his throat, determined to concentrate on researching Ruhin so they could get on with their mission—and then, ultimately, their lives.

He only wished he knew what that meant.

"So, did you find anything?"

Josie frowned, but her fingers continued to fly over the keyboard. "Nothing yet. Too bad there's not a database for evil, supernatural creatures."

"Who says there isn't?"

She glanced at him over her shoulder. "You're teasing, right?"

"Wish I was."

With no other option, he slid beside her on the couch. As if she'd smeared the candle wax over her skin, a fresh waft of woodsy scent played across his nostrils, luring him closer, invoking images in amber—lovemaking by candlelight. When she turned the laptop toward him and gazed with complete innocence, as if she had no idea of the power of her perfume, which he highly doubted, he hijacked the keyboard and went to his favorite search engine.

"I could use something to drink," he said.

She slid her hand across to the wineglasses they'd abandoned earlier.

"I think water would be better."

"Probably right," she replied.

While she filled two tall glasses with ice and water from the kitchen, Rick tried to remember the location of the site he'd found a few months ago. Written mostly in Latin and requiring a great deal of sloppy translation drawn from his first language, Spanish, he'd discovered little more than he already knew from the books. One thing about researching magical beings and lore—nothing much changed.

But he hadn't dug very deep and, since that time, hadn't had the opportunity to try and find the Web site again. The first time, he'd had to hack into it, following links from obscure bulletin boards and faking passwords and e-mail addresses and employing a few tricks he'd learned while on an Internet-crime task force a few years before.

Hunched over the laptop, he tried to retrace his steps, answering Josie's questions while he worked, trying to ignore the warmth of her skin beside his or how the scent of vanilla and musk that wafted into the air when she swung her hair into a twist on the back of her head, secured with the pencil she'd been using to take notes. Her questions ranged from the logical to the downright gruesome. Did ordinary people really believe there were vampires? Had he ever seen a ghost in a graveyard? Did the hag he'd encountered really have no face?

Despite the increasing goriness of his answers, Josie listened intently. Her voice remained both solid and soft, as if the topics did not frighten her. Clearly, she possessed a healthy dose of respect for not only what he'd accomplished, but for the creatures of the night they would soon confront. And the more she knew, the better.

He couldn't help wanting her to keep talking, keep whispering suggestions as he worked. The tone and volume were like a balm, keeping him calm and concentrated even as his searches for the elusive database came up empty.

But after an hour, he slid the laptop back onto the coffee table, stretched his arms and neck and yawned.

"I can't look at that thing anymore," he said. "The Web site is either down or moved. I can't even find the links. I give up. For tonight."

She closed the top. "It's not night anymore. Sun's up. Why don't we get some sleep?"

"Do you really think if we go to bed, we'll get any rest?" he asked.

She grinned slyly. "No."

He grabbed her hand. "Good, because neither do I."

11

UNDER THE SPELL of the scents Josie kept bringing into the bedroom in the form of candles or teas or wines she'd warmed and enhanced with herbs, they remained in bed all day, not even getting up to eat, but taking copious breaks to try the Internet again for the elusive database. If only they could find out more about their enemy, perhaps they'd have a chance in hell of beating him. Even without magic.

While Rick worked, Josie concocted a delicious soup. Once he was sure he'd again failed to find any information about Ruhin through the computer, they spooned mouthfuls of the hearty vegetable stew to each other while wrapped, naked, beneath the sheets that had been crisp and cool when they'd first fallen into them, but now melted around their bodies, wilted from the hot sex they'd shared well into the afternoon. That evening, while Josie showered, Rick stripped the bed, threw on a pair of jeans and forced open the window in the bedroom.

The air, though scented by the city, cleared his head. It was February and, while it had been warm for the past few days, the hint of rain filled the air. A hard downpour would soon pelt the heat into submission. He climbed out onto the fire escape and wrapped his arms tight across his bare chest. The gold crucifix he wore, a gift from his parents after graduating from the police academy, instantly chilled. He wore it for protection, much like Josie wore her bloodstone. Josie, who claimed to be nonmagical but had somehow managed to keep him under a powerful spell nonetheless. He didn't regret a single kiss or rapturous orgasm they'd shared since her reappearance in his life, but time was of the essence. With every moment he didn't pursue Ruhin, the more they were both in danger.

"Rick?"

He turned and poked his head through the wispy curtains. "Out here."

"Brr," she said. Her hair still damp at the edges, she climbed out onto the landing wearing nothing but a silky robe. The wind flapped the bottom and he caught sight of the sweet triangle of blond curls and a flash of the intimate lips he'd kissed as often as he'd kissed her mouth. He'd once considered her to be on the shy side, but Josie had surprised him. Pleasantly.

He helped her stand, then turned away from her, trying to ignore the intense sexual pull. He had to resist, or he'd never leave this apartment.

He figured that was her plan.

Clearly, it was working.

"We can't waste any more time," he said determinedly.

"Is that what we've been doing? Wasting time?" She slid her hands around him from behind, tucking her fingers into his arms with bold confidence, but her voice betrayed her uncertainty.

He cursed, then shifted and tugged until she was secure in his arms. Mixed with crisp night air, her hair smelled like heaven. Lavender and vanilla and musk and rain. If he didn't anticipate that the deluge was going to be freezing, he might have suggested they stay out there and let nature wash over them. But it was going to be nasty and cold. He'd lived in Chicago long enough to recognize the signs.

He took one more deep breath, then exhaled, loving the

sensation of her palms stroking up and down his back. "It's been too long since I've done anything but research and hunt demons. I haven't relaxed in months. I'm out of practice."

She chuckled. "You seemed to catch on pretty easily."

"Gracias a tu."

"De nada," she replied.

He scanned the alley underneath them, combing the dark recesses of the city streets for signs of his enemies. It was night and they'd been out in the open longer than was wise. Still, he couldn't suppress a wry grin at the window across the alley. The apartment dweller had decorated the pane with cardboard cutout cupids in fire-engine red, set off by a string of pink lights shaped like lips. They blinked in a rhythm that made him think that inside, music was playing.

"What song do you think those lips are set to?"

"Excuse me?"

He pointed out the window. She laughed, squeezed around him and cuddled in front. He groaned. How easy would it be for him to slip his hands into her robe and feel those luscious breasts again? Then they'd make love on the fire escape and lose another precious half hour in foreplay, sex and afterglow. He locked his hands around her waist in a pathetic attempt to resist.

"They're blinking to a song," he repeated.

"'Stupid Cupid'?" she guessed.

He laughed. "Could be. I never thought I'd be spending my first Valentine's Day with a serious lover planning to destroy a demon."

She turned in his arms. "Serious lover? What exactly does that mean?"

Had she not been looking up at him with such curiosity, he might have been able to think his way out of this discussion. He'd never been good at talking about the nature of his relationships, particularly with the woman in question. He preferred action to talk, but when he bent forward to attempt to sway the conversation, she placed her hand over his mouth, an effective barrier to distraction. She released him only when he pulled back.

"You're the one who let that demon out of the bag," she joked.

"I just wanted to say that I'd rather be combing through the Chicago guides to find the perfect romantic restaurant to take you to than searching for a database of ancient magical creatures and cults."

She grinned, accepting his explanation. "The St. Valentine myth is all about soldiers, though."

"Myth?" he asked, quirking an eyebrow.

She stared at him boldly. "Yes, myth. There were actually several *real* St. Valentines. None of them, as far as history is concerned, married soldiers secretly against the king's wishes before they went to battle. It's a good story, though. Sells a lot of greeting cards."

Rick swallowed thickly. The idea of binding his heart to Josie's before he confronted the demon he was destined to destroy would have been ridiculous to him a few days ago. Now, not so much. He could see himself fighting a whole hell of a lot harder if he knew he had her waiting for him on the other side of the dark path he'd have to follow. But he could never put her in that position. What if he didn't survive? How could he commit to her when the chance of making her a widow in the near future was so high?

Still, as much as he wanted to deny the truth, he and Josie had become more than friends—even more than lovers. On top of their comfortable repartee and incendiary lovemaking, he was starting to anticipate her actions and strategies as if she were his partner. Good cops knew their coworkers like the backs of their own hands. Just like he was getting to know Josie. Only knowing her was a lot more enjoyable and required a kind of physical stamina they didn't teach at the academy.

"I don't think we'll have time to shop for greeting cards anytime soon," Rick said finally, preferring to talk rather than contemplate the inevitable downward path of his relationship with Josie. Right now, they would both be better off focusing on the here and now.

"I like the handmade kind better, anyway."

Rick laughed. "The best I could do is a Post-it note with x's and o's on it."

"That would do," she said with a smile. "So a romantic dinner, huh? What else would be on the Valentine's Day agenda? If we weren't about to battle with a demon," she asked as she moved back toward the window, climbed through and then waited for him to join her.

"Here or in Chicago?"

"Chicago," Josie said quickly. "New York is great, but home is home."

"A boat ride on the Chicago River? A hansom cab ride down Michigan Avenue? Maybe a trip to Navy Pier? We could ride the Ferris wheel and make out all the way around."

"Sounds fabulous," she said, struggling to close the window just as the first sprinkles of rain splattered the glass. "We'll have to make a list for next year."

"If there is a next year," he said.

"Oh, yes. That defeatist attitude will come in very handy," she quipped. "You keep that up."

Rick grinned, acknowledging for the first time in forever that he enjoyed having someone to talk to, someone to joke with, someone to wrap his arms around and take his mind off his overwhelming urge to shout to the rooftops that magical creatures were, right this very moment, manipulating humans with their magic, inciting crime and executing anyone who got in their way. He'd always been aware, from the moment of his great-grandmother's vision, that he'd face great evil someday, but he'd told himself she'd meant all the criminals he'd put away as a cop. Still, he'd known he'd met his destiny the minute the shadow had attempted to take over his body six months ago.

Just as he'd known, only a few days before that at the police station, that quirky, unusual, free-spirited Josie would fit into the big roadmap of his life in a very similar way.

Once inside, Josie set about concocting a snack while he went back to the laptop and again tried to access the site he'd found once before. This time, he found an online library of ancient texts that referenced the occult. He found one reference to Ruhin and nearly shouted to Josie in triumph, until he realized the text only said that the faithful did not speak of him.

Apparently, the faithful also wrote the damned book, because that was the full breadth of the reference.

After another twenty minutes, he shut down the Internet connection, but not before letting out a string of curses that made Josie jump as she strolled toward him with a tray of food.

"Feel better?" she asked.

She slid sandwiches in front of him. He grabbed one and looked, trying to determine what she'd stuck inside.

"Relax. It's just peanut butter. I'm afraid I depleted my store of special herbs and potions."

He bit into the sandwich and was immediately reminded of home. Not Miami, of course. His mother would have gouged out her own eyes before she served her children something as strictly American as PB and J. Comfort food in the Fernandez casita was *pan Cubano y mantequilla,* a fancy name for butter on Cuban toast. But in his apartment in

Chicago, he'd often subsisted on quick-to-make meals of Jiffy with jelly. Guava jelly, usually. Less guilt that way.

"Need to make another trip to the witch doctor?"

She didn't reply and when he glanced over, he saw her teeth worrying her bottom lip.

"Josie?"

She turned, her blue eyes wide and innocent, as if she hadn't heard the last few things he'd said to her.

"What would you do? If I wasn't around?"

He grinned slyly, remembered how he'd slaked off his sexual urges all alone since leaving Chicago. "You really want details? Or should I just show you?"

The idea, while prurient, suddenly appealed to him a great deal. He realized that Josie wasn't on the same wavelength when she looked at him as if he'd sprung a second head.

Her expression shifted from confused to shocked to amused. "Later, Mr. Sex on the Brain."

"It's your fault," he claimed, raising his hands in mock innocence. "You're the one who keeps seducing me into staying put."

"And you're the one who keeps falling for it. Seriously, though. It's my laptop. You haven't been cyber-sleuthing for your information. How did you find the demons before I came?"

Rick frowned. He didn't mind telling Josie about the insidious undergrounds he'd discovered in every major city he'd visited, but he didn't want to show her. And he had a sinking suspicion she was about to suggest some hands-on detective work.

"Demons need to feed," he explained. "And they rarely attack people in the light, meaning, people who matter. They don't dive into suburban neighborhoods and attack soccer moms. Well, not generally, though there is this one case I heard of in California—"

Josie cut him off. "Okay, so they go for the homeless?"

"Deeper than that," he replied. "They go for the people who purposely live off the radar, who rarely come above ground, if you know what I mean."

Josie bit her bottom lip again. Yeah, she knew. Josie's mother had been a thief on the run from the law for a good portion of her childhood.

She grinned wryly. "Don't apologize. For one time in my life, maybe my less-than-traditional childhood will come in handy."

Rick slid his hand over hers. "This is more than just grifters and con men, Josie. This is serious stuff. Especially here in New York."

"Which means the network is huge and the population of people living on the other side even larger. Where would you start?"

He shrugged. "I'd hunt. Some demons can't help but come above ground, especially on the full moon. Generally, I'd find the creepiest part of town, usually near a cemetery and I'd just wait. Sooner or later, I'd catch sight of something and follow. Took time and planning, but—"

"We don't have either," Josie said.

"In a hurry to go back home?"

"What?" Her eyebrows shot up beneath her bangs and her eyes widened. Though she recovered quickly, Rick couldn't help wondering exactly what was going on in her mind right now. "Yes, I am. Aren't you?"

"There's nothing for me in Chicago anymore, Josie."

"I'm in Chicago."

"Not right now you're not."

"No, and I wish I was. If I was home, I'd know where to go."

"You know where the demons hang out in Chicago? Have you been holding out on me?" he said with a laugh in his voice, even though his chest tightened a fraction at the thought of Josie knowing more than she'd let on.

"No, of course not. It's just, well, you've been in my shop, right? You know what I sell. My customers are mostly dabblers, but I do get the occasional serious practitioner of the craft. They know I'm upscale, but I sell the genuine article. Rare stuff they can't find just anywhere. But I also get a lot of people coming in asking for potions to curse ex-boyfriends or candles that will shrivel their consciences so they can do things they wouldn't do otherwise."

"Black magic?"

She nodded. "I don't handle it, but I know who does. Sometimes, the black magic practitioners come into the shop, just to check me out. Make sure I'm not horning in on their territory, if you know what I mean."

Rick considered Josie's information, realizing she had a bead on a logical path to information. "Let's go back to that *botanica* we found in Spanish Harlem. Maybe the owner knows someone."

"It's too dangerous. The demon population might be looking for you, and I don't want to bring any grief down on her. She was really nice."

"So you want to go straight to the black magic source?"

"Definitely."

"How do we find them? Phone book?"

She snorted. "I suppose it's a start, but we could also ask around. New York's a big place, but the natives know their way around." Suddenly, she smiled. "We can ask Mario in the morning."

Rick arched a brow in question.

"The cab driver? He'll know. He knows everything about this city."

"Won't he think it's odd that we're asking?"

"Definitely. So we'd better come up with a really great story."

They ordered Chinese food and, amid chopsticks and

lemon chicken, came up with an explanation for their questions that Mario wouldn't find suspicious. And though Rick had suggested they go straight to sleep so they could be up early the next morning, they spent several delicious hours making love until just after midnight, when Josie curled her body against his and fell into a deep, dreamless sleep. Rick, on the other hand, fought persistent night terrors. Time and again, he awoke from yet another gory scene where he'd brought Josie into a dangerous situation he couldn't get her out of—and every time, he found the stupid amulet Regina had given Josie pressing hot against his back.

He exited the shower the next morning to find Josie buckling the strap on her boot, her damp hair tied back in a ponytail and her skin, fresh from her own shower in the other bathroom, glowing with excitement.

"Ready to get started?" she asked.

"I should probably dress first," he replied.

She smoothed out her dark jeans as she stood. "You look fine to me."

The hungry rumble in her voice made him hard, but Rick ignored the sensation and grabbed clean clothes from his duffel bag instead. "You're not exactly a fair judge when your sole purpose for the past two days has been to keep me naked and distracted."

"Are you complaining?"

"Not in the least."

"Good, then hurry up before I change my mind and drag you back into bed."

"Trust me, sweetheart. You wouldn't have to drag me."

With a giggle that lightened his soul, Josie popped out of the room and gave him time to dry his hair, then shrug into a long-sleeved, black T-shirt and similarly dark jeans. She was waiting for him by the door and together they descended the stairs and exited the building. As Josie predicted, though the sun wasn't up yet, Iris was stocking her cart, and her husband, Mario, was sitting on the hood of his cab, holding open a paper. As he'd predicted, the rain the night before had brought a wave of cold that was more in keeping with February weather. Josie zipped up her jacket and the sound caught Iris's attention.

"You're up early," Iris said when she saw them.

"That they're out of that apartment at all surprises me," Mario added slyly. He eyed Rick again with that assessing stare of his and Rick had to exercise all his control not to buckle under the scrutiny.

Josie entwined her arm with his. "Yeah, well, it's time for us to stock up on food and supplies before we go back underground again."

Rick shot her a shocked glare, but he realized from the cat-in-the-cream grin on her face that she meant the admission to come out as teasing and a little bit naughty.

Iris chuckled and wiggled her eyebrows. "Understandable. What can I get you?"

Rick laid a twenty on the counter of Iris's cart, gazed into the glass case and said, "Two guava turnovers, two café con leches and some information."

Mario cocked his head toward them but didn't move.

"What kind of information?" Iris asked, reaching for tongs and grabbing the *pasteles,* which she deposited skillfully in a white paper bag.

"I'm looking for a *botanica* or occult shop," Josie replied.

"You had a bag from one of those places the other day. The Crescent Moon," Mario said.

"You are observant," Josie admitted, blowing on the top of the café con leche Iris handed her.

Mario shrugged. "Old habits die hard."

"This time, we're looking for someplace a little more," she said, hesitating to find the right words, "well, off the beaten path."

"She's looking for someplace that specializes in dark magic," Rick clarified.

He didn't want to drag Iris and Mario into their problems, but they didn't have time to play coy.

"What for?" Iris asked hotly.

"We're looking for someone," Rick replied. "Someone who doesn't play nice in the occult world."

"Why do you think Iris would know where to find such a place?" Mario asked, sliding off his perch on the hood of the cab and closing the newspaper he'd been pretending to read.

Rick shoved his hands into his pockets. "She knows the city, doesn't she?"

"And she told me herself she knew a few fortune-tellers in her neighborhood," Josie continued. "If she knows the good places to go, she probably knows the—"

"Don't answer," Mario directed at his wife.

Clearly, Iris didn't like being ordered around, if the frown carving into her cocoa-colored skin was any indication. "Josie, who are you looking for?"

"We can't tell you," Josie replied. "I'm sorry. But we can't drag you into our drama."

"You dragged her in by asking," Mario insisted.

Josie passed a coffee to Rick, but he was too tense to take a sip. Mario's eyes, crinkled with age, assessed him with a scrutiny that Rick might have folded under in his younger days. The old taxi driver reminded Rick suddenly of his father. Kindhearted and jovial one minute, intimidating and formidable the next. Better to make him a friend rather than an enemy. Rick already had enough of those.

He nodded his head to the side, indicating that he and

Mario should go off and talk a few minutes on their own. Mario complied and, while he heard Iris complain in the background about men in general, they strolled down the sidewalk and, for a few silent moments, watched the sunlight spill from behind the tall buildings.

"What do you know about magic, Mario?"

"I like that David Copperfield guy. Saw him on television once. Made the Statue of Liberty disappear, just like that." He ended with a snap.

Despite his words, Rick knew Mario didn't believe that magic was real. Probably wouldn't believe it was real even if he saw it with his own eyes.

"You know there are people who believe they can do magic, right? Not stage stuff, but real magic. Voodoo. Santería."

"Yeah, I know all about that crap. I was a cop, remember? Right here in NYC. One trip into Crown Heights in the nineties can convince you anything exists."

Rick didn't know the difference between Crown Heights and Queens. He hadn't been in New York long enough to know all the boroughs and neighborhoods. But if Crown Heights was anything like Miami's Little Haiti, then Mario understood where he was coming from.

"That's what we're looking for. Someone who's into that shit."

Mario eyed him skeptically. "Those people can be dangerous."

Rick stood up straighter and met Mario's gaze with his own private brand of determination. "Do I look like I can't take care of myself?"

"What about Josie? She's not exactly Wonder Woman. Iris and I haven't known her long, but we don't want to see her hurt."

"Neither do I."

Mario gave a nod, and then turned so they could walk back

to the cart. A few customers had come up, but surprisingly, it was Josie who was mixing their coffees and doling out doughnuts. Iris was hunched over a nearby mailbox, drawing on a white napkin. The customers left as Mario and Rick approached.

"Here you go," Iris said. "The place is hard to find, but there's this guy, hangs out on the corner, named Shining Jim. Take him this box of *pasteles* and tell him I said hello to his *tia* Luli. He'll take you the rest of the way."

"We can trust him?" Rick asked, snatching the paper out of Josie's hand and earning an annoyed frown from her.

Iris laughed. "Not as far as you can throw him, and he weighs about three hundred pounds, so that's not far. But he'll take you to this store for my pastries. Besides, he's afraid of his *tia* Luli and we used to get our hair done at the same place."

"And the owner is into the black arts?" Josie asked.

Iris shook her head. "No, I don't think so. Not seriously. Maybe she does a little voodoo on cheating boyfriends or makes up jujus to curse a noisy neighbor, but nothing like what you're looking for. But I've seen the crowd who comes into her shop. If she doesn't know about the dark arts, someone around there will."

12

MARIO INSISTED on driving them and, to be honest, Josie was glad. Mario knew New York City like the back of his slightly arthritic hand. He found the corner Iris had directed them to and waited while they talked to Shining Jim, so named because he wore more gold jewelry than Mr. T in the eighties.

Even his teeth were rimmed with metal, though he hardly opened his mouth as he pointed them to the alley that would lead them to the shop they sought.

With a wave at Mario, Rick and Josie set off.

This corner of Crown Heights hadn't experienced the gentrification of the rest. Old buildings lined the alleyway they walked down and the strong odors of rotting garbage, mold and urine caused Josie to tug the collar of her jacket closer around her nose. The rain began again, even icier than before. With the gray clouds crowding the sky, she wondered if the quick drop in temperature might mean snow. Just as her jacket started to saturate with rainwater, they found the black-windowed storefront. The only indication of the store's purpose was the neon-lit eye on the door and a pentagram etched into a block of wood tacked above it.

"Ready?" Rick asked, his hand on the knob.

She gave a quick, cold nod and pressed Regina's amulet. It had warmed the minute they'd exited Mario's taxi and though she felt a minuscule spike when bells announced their entrance, she wondered if her trepidation was causing her imagination to run rampant. She had to concentrate on gathering information. Nothing else mattered. It had been a long time since she'd had to pull off a quick escape on a moment's notice, but she guessed the skill might be a lot like riding a bike.

"Hello?"

Muffled voices from the back of the tiny shop stilled.

"Who's there?" a woman asked, her accent distinctly Caribbean.

"Josie Vargas," Josie replied. "Iris sent me. She said you might be able to help me out."

The woman came out from around the corner, a red-and-gold head wrap covering her hair, though the dreadlocked ends sprang from the top like water from an inky fountain. With a matching caftan draped artfully over her tall, slim body, she was everything Josie expected—except not.

"Iris who?"

Josie came up short. She had no idea what Iris's last name was. "She owns the pastry cart downtown?"

The woman gave a quick nod, her eerie green-gold eyes honing in on Rick. "Who are you?"

"Her escort," he said, giving Josie a nod. They'd decided in the cab over that Josie was going to do most of the talking. While Rick knew the jargon and vocabulary of magic just as well as Josie by now, he didn't want to draw too much attention to himself in case the demons looking for him had put the word out among the mundane followers of dark magic.

The woman smiled. "Smart girl to bring some impressive muscle with her to this part of town. Iris never sends me customers. What can I help you with?"

Josie pulled a list from the pocket of her jeans. "Some things I need."

She handed the scrap paper to the woman, along with a fifty-dollar bill, which would cover the cost of her supplies and then some. The woman leaned over to a nearby lamp to get a better look. "I have all this," she said, and her voice held a tinge of skepticism. "But you could get these items at any occult shop. Why venture into the darkness for such innocent items?"

Josie acknowledged the woman's suspicions with a nod. "That's just what I want to buy. I also need something you might not necessarily have for sale," she explained, handing the woman a second fifty. She and Rick didn't have unlimited cash, so they'd decided to be frugal. She could only hope it would be enough.

"Like?" the woman asked, eyes narrowed.

"Information," Rick said.

The woman arched a brow, and a quick glance over her shoulder revealed that whomever she'd been speaking to earlier had come out from behind the partition.

"Who you?" the man asked.

He was tall and nearly as wide. He made Shining Jim look like an action figure.

Josie stepped between Rick and the man. If there was one thing she knew about all things occult, it was that the women often took the leadership role. It was just one of the aspects of her belief system that she loved.

"Never mind who he is," she said, forcing bravado into her voice that she did not feel, and turning her gaze back to the woman in the head scarf. "Are you interested in hearing me out or just trying to intimidate me?"

Not surprisingly, the woman gave the huge bulk of a man a dismissive nod. He sneered once more in their direction and then disappeared in the back of the store.

"What kind of information are you looking for?" the woman asked.

"We're actually looking for another store or gathering place, somewhere frequented by those who practice the black arts."

The woman shook her head furiously. "I don't do no black magic here. Bad juju, that."

Josie scanned the shelves, noticing more than a fair amount of fetishes and symbols she would never have allowed in her own shop. But this dark magic paraphernalia was pretty standard fare. What they were looking for was darker, more taboo, particularly in the Wiccan world. She might not even recognize it when she saw it.

"I didn't say you did," Josie said. "But Iris said you know everyone who teaches the craft in the city. You'd know where to find what I need."

The woman stepped forward, her green gaze stabbing her with its lack of patience. "What do you need, exactly?"

"Ruhin," Josie replied.

The woman's dark skin paled. "Get out."

Rick grabbed Josie's hand and tugged her behind him.

"The name means something to you?"

The woman grabbed a nearby shelf for balance. Her monstrosity of a friend reappeared and they exchanged a few words in Creole, which Josie did not understand.

"You leave now," the man insisted.

"Just tell us what you know," Josie pleaded. "All we have is a name. We need more."

"Forget that name," the woman insisted, terror in her eyes. "Don't speak it aloud again unless you want to bring up the wrath of the underworld. That's an old name. An evil name." She grabbed a bottle of red liquid, pulled out the stopper and handed it to Josie. "Swish this into your mouth. Spit out the name. But outside. Not in here. I cannot allow that evil into my shop. Do it!"

Josie took the bottle and Rick led them out the door. As the woman watched, horror-struck, Josie did as she asked, filling her mouth with the liquid that tasted of dandelion root, garlic and—she nearly gagged—blood. Spitting it out on the grimy ground came naturally. As she completed the ritual, she expected the woman to tell them more. Instead, she grabbed the bottle from Josie, went inside her shop and bolted the door.

She cursed and spit again behind her hand. Wasn't the most attractive thing she could do in front of Rick, but the vile drink coated her tongue and she feared if she didn't expectorate the taste soon, she'd retch. Rick was over her in a minute, rubbing her back and whispering his condemnation of her actions in the sweetest voice possible.

"I was trying to earn her trust," she explained.

"You could have ended up dead," he pointed out.

A high-pitched but male voice echoed from beside a broken public phone hanging haphazardly on the wall. "Dead from that *bruja?*" The kid snorted. "She's harmless. Talks a good game. Showy and shit, but she's not where the real power is."

Rick stood and positioned himself between Josie and the teen. "And you know the location of this 'real power'?"

"Shit, yeah."

"Then why are you hanging around here, listening in to conversations that are none of your business?"

The door to the occult shop swung open and a half second later, the woman in the head scarf had the teen by the scruff of the neck. "Because he's a good-for-nothing wannabe." She started cursing at him in her native tongue, but the teen, who looked red-haired and blue-eyed underneath the black pharmacy dye job and thick, kohl eyeliner, seemed to understand every word. In fact, he argued back at her for a moment until her mountain of a companion shoved himself through the door.

"You go now!" the woman bellowed, tossing the teenager like a rag doll into her companion's waiting arms. "There ain't nothing good to come of the questions you're asking. Get out, before I make you go."

Rick started to argue, but Josie placed her hand on his shoulder and compelled him forward with a pointed look. When they passed the teenager, he struggled to get loose and something went flying out of his pocket. Rick pretended to stumble, palmed the item and then hurried Josie out of the alley.

Only after they cleared the protection of the buildings did Josie realize how cold it had become. And how wet. The rain now sluiced down from a leaden sky. Shining Jim and his cohorts were no longer lazing around at the corner, and the only people on the sidewalks were moving fast and with newspapers or cardboard boxes over their heads for protection. The cars on the streets seemed to realize that being out in this weather wasn't a good idea, so they shot by at top speed. Josie kept her head down, wincing as icy drops of rain slid down the back of her collar and only looked up when Rick let out a surprised, "Well, I'll be damned."

Mario tooted the horn of his cab, then slid up to the curb so they could dash inside.

"Thought I told you not to wait," Rick said irritably.

"Bet you're damned glad I don't listen," the cabbie replied, tossing a couple of rough, woolen blankets into the back seat. They smelled stale and musty, but at least they were dry. Josie dabbed her face dry and then leaned over to attack her hair so, at the very least, she wouldn't have cold drops slinking down the back of her neck.

Rick, on the other hand, was looking at what she assumed was the item dropped by the kid in black.

"What is it?"

"An address and a time."

He tilted the scrap of paper toward her so she could read

today's date, an address that meant nothing to her and a notation that read, "11:45 p.m."

"Not midnight? That would be creepier."

He smirked. "Maybe they need fifteen minutes to set up."

"Set up what?" she asked.

He flipped the paper over. The words *mano izquierda* were scrawled on the other side.

The necklace around Josie's neck warmed. "Left hand? This isn't good."

Rick nodded. He understood. In his research of the occult, he'd clearly run across references to the Left Hand Path. Diametrically opposed to the white ways of the Wiccans, who followed the credo of, "First, do no harm," the Left Hand Path had no doctrine or philosophy to guide its followers, which often included Satanists. They existed only for their own interests, often prurient and nearly always self-gratifying. Rick had met more than his fair share of followers and they were always creepy. If not dangerous.

He instinctively placed his hand over the crucifix. "I have a bad feeling about this."

Josie smirked. "Ruhin. Left Hand Path. Bad feelings. Sounds like we're on the right track."

They rode the rest of the way in silence, though from the frequency of Mario's peeks into his rearview, Josie guessed he wanted to know what was going on. She considered asking for his help, but the thought of putting anyone else in danger convinced her otherwise. Instead, she thanked him with a kiss on the cheek when he pulled up outside their building and she insisted he take the money Rick offered him for the ride.

They went back up to the apartment in silence, stripping out of their wet clothes and tossing them into the tiny apartment dryer so they could be worn again tonight. Josie turned the knob and pressed the On switch, soothed for a moment by the hum and clink of the clothes as they spun in the increasing heat. After a few minutes, she felt Rick behind her. His chilly hands tickled at first, but as he rubbed her thighs, stomach and buttocks, they warmed with the same intensity as her insides.

She turned into his chest and, in the twilight darkness of the stormy afternoon, explored his body as if learning every nook and cranny might help her keep him safe tonight. His thighs had sinews and curves she outlined with her fingers and his buttocks were a testament to artistry. She ran her hands through the coarse hair on his arms and sprinkled around his nipples, which she noticed had hardened like bullets, begging for her tongue. She traced the gold chain he wore, marveling at the contrast of the bright metal against his dark skin. His chin, so square and angled, utterly intoxicated her. And his eyes. Even as she smoothed her fingertips over his closed lids, she knew she could willingly lose herself in his jet-black irises, which darkened to unfathomable when his gaze met hers again with a hunger like no other she'd ever seen.

The sensitive spots were saved for last. Groans of pleasure intermingled with coaxing coos the minute his fingers tested her readiness and found her as wet and warm as he was hard and hot. He lifted her onto the top of the small dryer and eased her legs apart, then guided her feet and knees upward, opening her completely to him. The heat of the machine beneath her bottom intensified as the head of his penis pressed deep inside.

But he did not pump into her. Instead, he kissed her, eyes open, hand dancing around the edges of her face in silent veneration. His mouth, when not driving her mad with kisses, tilted into an intense and serious frown.

She touched the sides of his mouth. "What's wrong?"

"You're so beautiful," he said.

"I'm sorry," she said.

He did not laugh at her joke.

"I don't want you to get hurt," he insisted.

"I know," she reassured, sliding her fingers through his hair. "Contrary to popular belief, I don't want to get hurt, either."

She scooted forward on the dryer. Her skin was starting to burn, both on the outside from the temperature of the machine and on the inside, with Rick so hard and heavy in her, but not creating the friction she needed so desperately.

"Then don't go with me tonight."

She kissed him, grabbed his bicep and pulled him forward until he was in to the hilt. He hissed, dragging his hands down her back.

"Josie, you—" he started, but she placed her hands on his cheeks and kissed him with every ounce of her need. He wasn't going to convince her to let him go without her and she wasn't going to stand for this cruel and unusual punishment for one second longer.

He slipped his hands underneath her. "You're burning up," he panted.

"You have no idea," she replied. "Now finish what you started, or I'll go insane."

He complied. Hungrily. Willingly. Completely. The motion and heat beneath her and inside her drove her to orgasm almost instantly, but Rick held out. He lifted her off the dryer and dropped into a nearby chair.

The pure decadence incited her desire yet again. With his cooling touch on her backside and his lips curving around her nipples, she braced her feet on the floor and locked her hands behind his neck. The leverage was exquisite, allowing her to control the depth of his thrusts and the tightness of her body around his. In no time, she was on the verge of climax again, and this time, he tumbled with her, shouting out her name in a strangled sound that made her realize just how much he wanted to resist her—and just how much he could not.

"I won't lose you," he said, his breath ragged.

She laid her head on his shoulder, inhaling the deliciously salty scent of his skin. "No, you won't."

"You make me feel like I can take on the world."

"I don't want to make you feel that way," Josie admitted. "Besides, it's not the world that has me scared. It's the underworld I'm worried about."

"Then don't come with—"

She placed her fingers over his lips.

His dark eyes showed his surrender. He slipped her fingers into his mouth and suckled, torturing her mercilessly.

"I propose we use this weather to our advantage," he said, when he had her pressing hard against him once more.

The idea of making love again in the cold rain after this super-hot encounter appealed to her. "Yes, let's."

He kissed her nose, lifted her off him and headed to the dryer to retrieve their clothes. She couldn't help the way her mouth watered when he bent down, his hard ass so perfectly round, his manly bits dangling.

"That's not what I meant," he said, spinning around and catching the obviously lusty look on her face. "We need to get to that address early and stake the place out. We need to know what sort of thing that kid is leading us to."

She slid into the chair, draping her exhausted limbs over the armrest. "Back to business, huh?"

"Do you want to go back to Chicago anytime soon?"

"You know I do. But," she started, then braced herself for an answer she didn't want to hear. "What about you?"

He looked away and busied himself with buttoning his jeans. "I can't make any promises, Josie. I can only concentrate on finishing what I've started. After that, I'm not sure." He spun around as he shrugged into his T-shirt.

She supposed she shouldn't ask for more. The truth was, she loved it in Chicago. Her business, her friends, the only stability and routine she'd ever known was in the Windy City. She'd lived just about everywhere else and she'd never had roots, never really fit in until she'd shunned her mother's vagabond existence, reclaimed the family building she now had her shop in and made a life for herself that was entirely her own. She couldn't imagine ever leaving.

But Rick had nothing left. He'd destroyed his career by disappearing. Any friendships he might have had off the force had likely tanked too. She'd been in contact with his family but, to her knowledge, no one else had. He'd have her, but she had no illusions that that would be enough. Rick was a man who embraced purpose, as evidenced by his actions since his first run-in with the demon soul. Once he'd done what he set out to do, he'd have a serious reexamination of his life to do, and she wasn't sure where—or if—she'd fit in.

Once dressed, Rick held out his hand to Josie, a devastatingly sexy smile brightening his face, making her dark thoughts fade away. "Let's do it."

Pouting, she shrugged into her lingerie. "We already did it. Twice. And it was very nice. Though one more time for the road wouldn't be such a bad thing."

She'd looked away to hide her disappointment, then screamed when he scooped her up into his arms with an evil laugh and carried her to bed.

13

RICK TOOK A DEEP BREATH, hoping the cold air in his lungs would reinvigorate his sexually exhausted body. From the moment she'd come back into his life, he'd wanted nothing more than to make love to Josie twenty-four hours a day. If he took the time to do the math, he might have actually come close. But now they had a link to Ruhin or, at the very least, to the type of people who would know more about him, and he had to banish any lusty thoughts from his mind.

In between lovemaking, Rick had listened to Josie's information about the Left Hand Path. She'd told him very little he hadn't already learned from his own research, but the fear he'd heard in her voice had been enough for him to consider, yet again, some scheme to leave her behind—premonition be damned. Unfortunately, she already knew the address, so short of tying her up or locking her in a closet, he'd feared she'd show up anyway. So there they were, staking out what looked like an abandoned warehouse for the second time that day. First, they'd come by in the afternoon with Mario to get the lay of the land, finding the entire area not only deserted, but the inside guarded by at least two nasty dogs that looked like Doberman–pit bull mixes.

Now, an hour before the appointed hour, they'd returned, this time by bus. Rick used the cold front to their advantage, lighting a fire in a drum container near the corner. With both of them dressed in hooded sweatshirts and coats they'd picked up from a secondhand store, they blended into the downtrodden neighborhood. Across from him, Josie had her gloved hands above the fire, but her gaze was entirely lost in the flames. Worry lines creased the pale skin on her temples and her mouth, a luscious, natural pink, curved into an anxious frown.

Even in the damp and dirty clothes, with her hair tied back and her shoulders hunched against the cold, she was beautiful. He had no business dragging her out into this frosty, wet weather, no business involving her in the dangerous pit his life had become. Try as he could to lock on to some sort of future with her in Chicago, he couldn't think that far ahead. Even if they did triumph over the demon and make it out alive, Rick had nothing left in the city but bad memories and a trashed reputation. No, if he went anywhere, it would be back to Miami. But could he really leave Josie behind?

At that moment, she looked up at him. The determination in her eyes, as well as confident smile, fueled a sudden calm. She was a remarkable woman. Amazing. Sexy, intelligent, resourceful and determined. She'd built a successful business literally from nothing, in a building someone in her income bracket couldn't ordinarily afford to rent, much less own. And yet, she'd dropped everything to seek him out and help him fight his demon. He had no right to ask her to leave everything behind, but if they made it that far, he knew he would. And he knew he'd be devastated if she refused.

The sound of tires on gravel caught his attention.

"Here they come."

A line of cars, some old and battered, others shiny and top-of-the-line, pulled into the rutted parking lot. The lead car—a banged-up Honda—waited at a rusted roll-up door at the warehouse, which suddenly crept up to allow them entrance. Before the automatic door dolled down, they saw about ten or twelve people dressed in jeans and a variety of dark blue or black climb out of the cars and shuffle into the darkness. None of the windows flared with any light, but that wasn't surprising. Most, if not all, had been blacked out from the inside.

"Did you see our little friend?" he asked Josie.

She shook her head. "I guess he could have been any of them. We need to get closer."

"Why don't I go in, pretend to want to join their ceremony?"

"What if they don't allow walk-ins?"

"The kid dropped that card on purpose, I'm sure of it. And if he didn't, it's enough of a cover story to get me inside. If I get into trouble, you can use your jewelry to call in reinforcements," Rick suggested.

Josie looked at him as if he'd lost his mind. "The minute I call Regina, that's the end, you know that, right?"

He nodded. Not that he planned on letting the regal, bossy witch determine the path of his future, but the truth remained that with her extraordinary powers, he might not have a choice.

"Do what you have to," he replied.

He turned to walk across the street, but Josie's hand shot out and grabbed him at the wrist. "You need to be careful, Rick."

Because this time, I'm with you.

She didn't say the words. She didn't have to. He knew the stakes. Knew the risks. A week ago, he would have boldly finessed his way inside and, using his bravado and bulk, would have extracted the information he needed without a single care if someone knifed him in the back or put a hole in his heart with an illegal firearm. He'd only cared about doing the job. If that had meant putting his life on the line for a cause he didn't fully understand, so be it. He wasn't about to be haunted or hunted by a demon soul for the rest of his life.

But now, he had Josie to worry about. Luckily for him, his training on the force had not deserted him, though his "spot a cop in a heartbeat" look had fallen by the wayside. He rubbed his stubbled chin, winked at Josie and started across the street. After he crossed, she followed.

He pointed at a window a floor up that had a sliver of light showing near the pane. She nodded and proceeded to a tall Dumpster around the corner. She might be able to see inside from there. He waited until she'd climbed up, peeked in and gave him a silent thumbs-up before he opened the side door and walked in.

He was stopped immediately by a lanky woman in a grimy T-shirt and torn ski jacket. "Who are you?"

"Does it matter?" he replied.

"You've got no business here," she said with a sneer.

He pulled the slip of paper out of his pocket and flicked it at her. "This says I do."

"Who gave you this?" she challenged.

"I did," came a voice from behind.

It was the kid. He wasn't cowering anymore and, in the light from several camping-type lanterns and flashlights strung around the central area of the cavernous warehouse, he looked fit and strong. "He's the guy who was asking about Ruhin at my aunt's shop."

The woman glared at him, but her eyebrows, studded with silver, rose with a measure of respect. "Got balls, coming here," she replied, and he finally identified her accent as British.

Rick flashed his best smile. "I've got more than that, but this isn't the time or the place."

All the tension the Brit chick had shown when he'd first shown up immediately slithered out of her, replaced by a hungry look that made his skin crawl. She patted him on the shoulder and nodded toward the big room, where people were milling around what Rick could now identify as a makeshift altar.

"My name's Kick," the kid said.

"For real?" Rick asked.

"Nah, but I kick a lot of ass, so that's what everyone calls me," he said proudly.

Rick smelled the distinct odor of teenage hyperbole, but he didn't call the kid on it. While tall, the teen was skinny as a reed and probably wouldn't last two seconds with someone who weighed more than the average woman.

"Come on," Kick said. "Party's just starting."

Someone had brought a couple of six-packs, the cans still cool, as if they'd just been jacked from the nearest convenience store. Rick instinctively swiped his sleeve around the edge of the metal, popped the top and took a swig.

"Clean up too much and you'll miss out on all the fun," Kick said, slapping him on the shoulder.

"Clean what up?"

The kid gestured toward his beer. Rick's chest tightened. He'd figured it was safe to drink a beer that clearly hadn't been opened, but Kick's warning implied otherwise.

Seconds later, the kid's warning made sense. Rick turned toward the fire and his eyes shimmied as if loose in their sockets. He squeezed his lids shut and wondered what the hell the bastards had slipped him.

"It's a hell of a rush," Kick said, licking the top of his can before chugging his beer. "Stole the shit from my aunt's store."

Rick spit on the ground and wiped his mouth, which made the kid laugh.

"Don't sweat it, man. It's all natural. Some fucking root or vine or crap. It won't kill you, but you'll see worlds you didn't know existed."

Rick swallowed thickly, then wiped his mouth again. "I'm more interested in this world, thanks."

The room upended for a second, then settled down. He couldn't have ingested too much of whatever the kid had dusted over the beer can, but even a tiny hit was taking him off his game. He was damned glad Josie was still outside.

"Haven't you done this before?" Kick asked, a sudden suspicious slant to his eyes.

"Why would you think that?"

"You came in asking about Ruhin. No one knows about him but the left-handers. You saw how my aunt reacted. She plays it up that she's all about the dark magic to get people in her shop to pay her for jujus and curses, but she's full of shit. All talk. This is where the real shit happens. You watch."

Rick's mouth started to water involuntarily and the firelight suddenly seemed brighter. More intense. His balance wavered, but he recovered with a hand to the kid's shoulder.

"Yeah," he said. "Can't wait. Till it starts though, what do you know about Ruhin? Ever seen him?"

"Man, with this stuff, you see everything!"

Beckoned by one of his friends, the kid walked away and joined the band of drinkers nearest to the fires they'd lit in twin drums on either side of an altar; it looked more like an old metal door bolted to sturdy crates than anything particularly religious or sacred. Rick glanced around, counting ten people in the room. Only two were women, including the pierced chick who'd accosted him at the door. The rest were men, boys really. Kick was the youngest, but not by much.

Made sense, he supposed. Teens were always experimenting with crap they didn't understand. Probably thought it was cool to be fucking around with the occult, not knowing they were mixed up with real demons who would rip their throats out with the least incentive.

Mustering all of his concentration, Rick strolled across the room, draining the beer on the floor as he walked. He stood just behind Kick and his friends, taking the appropriate place of an outsider who wasn't trying too hard and listened to them talk about all the supposedly wild shit they'd done all week. Nothing seemed connected to the paranormal. Sounded more like a bunch of punks stealing for drug money or working off their frustrations on public property than anything else.

He turned to make a reconnaissance sweep around the room when the pierced woman caught him by the collar of his jacket.

"Where you going?" she asked silkily.

"Out to take a piss," Rick replied, hoping his crassness would send her on her way. "Beer went right through me."

But instead of giving him his space, she slithered closer. "I hear some freaks like to get pissed on while they're having sex. You're not one of those, are you?"

Rick fought to keep a disgusted sneer off his face. This had been a mistake. These people were wannabes attracted to the life because of the counterculture and lurid side effects, not because they knew anything about the real evil power loose in the world. He couldn't play protector to a bunch of strung-out kids. He had to concentrate on keeping himself alive—and Josie.

He flicked her fingers off his clothes. "Not even remotely."

He managed only two steps around her before she latched onto his arm. "Still, if you're going to whip it out and everything, we might as well take advantage, right?"

"You don't even know me."

"I know you're not high, except on that shit Kick thinks it's funny to blow on the beer cans. I know you've taken a bath in the last twenty-four hours. That's more than I can say for the rest of these assholes."

"Just call me Mr. Perfect," he said.

She flicked out her tongue excitedly, clearly interpreting his humor as an invitation to wrap her hand around his arm and tug him toward the door. "I'm Dizzy, by the way."

Rick had no desire to give her his name. Not even a fake one. "It's that stuff Kick is handing out. Packs a punch."

She laughed. "No, my name. Dizzy. You can call me Dizz."

"That's great, Dizz, but don't you have some sort of ceremony to get ready for?"

When they reached the exit, she glanced over her shoulder. The guys gathered around the fire were laughing raucously and Kick was no longer hiding his stash, but was sprinkling the powder on his beer can and encouraging everyone to take a lick. Rick's stomach turned, but then Dizz flattened her slim body against his and kissed him. Well, it wasn't really a kiss. More like the forced shoving of a tongue down his throat. A tongue with metal accoutrements.

"Whoa," he said.

"Don't you want to do me? Before everyone else does?"

"Is that what this is? Some kind of fucking orgy?"

She shrugged. "It's whatever he wants it to be."

"Who?" Rick asked.

She stepped back and Rick realized he might have made a mistake.

"Don't you know?"

"Look," Rick said. "Kick just invited me. Slipped me a scrap of paper with the time and location before his aunt grabbed him by his ear and dragged him back into her shop."

"What were you doing there, if not looking for a party?"

"Looking for information."

Her hand slid down her jeans, to a pocket he guessed held some sort of weapon. "What kind of information? You a cop?"

"Not anymore. Not for a long fucking time. I'm traveling the Left Hand Path now. I got sick of fighting for the so-called good guys and watching my buddies get their jollies beating some perp to a bloody mess and then having to cover it up."

That lie he'd used before, just in case anyone decided to check up on him. Because in many ways, it wasn't a lie at all.

"You don't like beating the crap out of people?" she asked.

Rick knew what his answer had to be. "I don't like covering it up."

He injected just enough of a sinister tone into his voice to erase any doubts the woman had, but she didn't release him and, when he reached for the door, seemed doubly anxious to accompany him outside. Just then, a pop sounded behind them and when they turned, sparks were flying from the center of the altar, arcing upward in streaks of purple and red.

"Shit," she said. "It's starting."

"Yeah, well, orgies aren't my thing. I'm out of here."

"No," she whined. "You don't have to do anything. Stand back and watch. Bet you won't be able to resist joining in once the action heats up."

Dizzy ran into center of the warehouse, where the rest of the unfaithful were forming a circle around the altar. Rick weighed his options, glancing at the blacked-out window in the door, wondering where Josie was and what she'd seen. Dizzy seemed to know considerably more than Kick, who was probably just a poser rebelling against his overbearing auntie. Rick had absolutely no desire to witness Dizzy getting it on with any of the men in the room, much less more than one, but the party was just getting started and his chance to learn more about Ruhin might go up in smoke if he didn't act now.

Clearly, the name wasn't unknown to this group and they didn't seem to fear it the way the woman in the occult shop had. He had an opportunity here he couldn't let pass, even when he noticed how he was sweating and how blinking rapidly didn't really clear his eyesight as it had before.

He walked back into the cavernous room, though he remained on the fringes of the circle. Dizzy and the other woman positioned themselves on either side of the altar. They stripped off their tops, then dabbed their fingers into small cups positioned at the corners of the table and smeared a bloodred coloring over their protruding nipples, each enhanced by metal rods and piercings. Bracing their hands on the tabletop, they threw back their heads and jutted out their chests, as if in offering.

The men, arms raised but hands not touching, completed a circle around them. They were chanting in low tones and the words, nonsensical, seemed to get louder with each repetition. Rick heard a sudden, powerful drumming from the shadows. Was someone else there?

The sparks flew again and instinctively Rick reached for the Taser he'd tucked beneath his jacket. He caught himself. A weapon would give him away. He was not here to hunt but to watch. To learn.

Smoke started to spiral up from the altar, with no discernible source. The smell was putrid and eerily familiar. It was the odor of a demon kill. Rotting flesh, fired to a charred crisp. Whatever was coming, it wasn't human. And no matter how young this coven, they'd invoked something truly evil.

The tendrils of smoke curled into a form. Definitely male and definitely brawny. The skin on the naked creature stretched tight and gleamed, as if oiled. From the muscular structure, Rick knew suspected it wasn't a demon, but then was proved wrong when he spied the burn mark at the center of the throat. Its eyes possessed an eerie glow in a purplish blue that reminded Rick of a black light.

"Come closer, my lovelies," the demon said, holding out a hand to Dizzy and her friend in turn. They climbed sensually onto the altar and rubbed their bodies against him. He flicked a finger across their lips and instantly, their eyes dilated to total blackness and they dropped to their knees.

They were under his control in ways Rick had never witnessed. He'd seen so much, but never the enslavement of humans by a magical creature.

This wasn't good. Not good at all.

14

JOSIE HELD HER BREATH and, in her mind, concentrated on two things: standing motionless and filling her mind with the full text of the Wiccan law as she'd learned it. She had to keep her thoughts occupied. Her body still.

Perfectly still.

Bide the Wiccan law ye must, in perfect love, in perfect trust. Eight words the Wiccan rede fulfill: an ye harm none, do as ye will. And ever mind the rule of three: what ye send out, comes back to thee. Follow this with mind and heart, and merry ye meet, and merry ye part.

After the fifth recitation, the footsteps she'd heard below a few moments ago, accompanied by the acrid scent of tobacco, drifted away.

Perched atop a pile of debris, she willed herself to breathe again. She was not giving herself away. Unlike the female co-stars of too many action movies, she wasn't going to allow her klutzlike tendencies to get her and Rick into more trouble. She was a witch, damn it. Mundane or not, she'd come far in searching for Rick when he didn't want to be found and she'd helped him get into a ceremony with a group of people who were clearly Left Hand Path—the precise type of practitioners that someone in the service of Ruhin would gravitate toward.

Through a chiseled gap between a window and the frame, she'd watched the action unfold below, practically twisting herself into a pretzel shape to spy on Rick when the sleazy bitch at the door had attempted to win a game of tonsil hockey. Then she'd heard the footsteps and opted to do a statue imitation until the person lingering below had left. Now, she turned to look back inside the building again, but her view was blocked by a haze of colored smoke.

The heart-shaped necklace she'd tucked against her skin buzzed with warning. When it flared, she cursed and, through her shirt, pulled it away from her chest. Was she in danger again this time or was Rick? Or perhaps, both of them?

Carefully, she hunched down, then, lying flat on her stomach, peeked over the ledge. The alley was dark but empty. Behind her, she could hear voices from inside the building. Chanting. Loud declarations in an ancient tongue. Spoken with increasing urgency, the incantation broke through the cracks in the wall and chilled her blood to the marrow of her bones. She scrambled down the makeshift lookout then, keeping herself as flat against the wall and shrouded in shadow as she could, made her way to the door.

Surprisingly, the door was unlocked. Her fear increased.

Every Wiccan she knew operated in the open air when they could. Yes, she'd attended ceremonies indoors, of course, but the important rituals relied on the powerful pull of natural forces. Since this group was Left Hand, she hadn't blinked at their working in this run-down warehouse, but to leave the door unlocked meant they didn't care who walked in. Or someone had made a very sloppy mistake.

She opened the door barely half an inch, trying to see through the crack, but her vision was angled away from the fire she'd seen from above. She'd have to go inside. At least the smoke would provide her with cover. Sucking in a deep breath, she eased the door open and slid inside, flush against the wall.

A second later, her shoulder bumped something hard but pliant.

Like someone else's arm.

She nearly screamed, but a hand flew around her mouth. The person's scent immediately hit her.

Rick.

"What are you doing?" he muttered into her ear, dragging her into the shadows before she could see what was going on ahead of them.

"Checking on you," she replied, once they were hidden behind a stack of rotting crates. "What's—"

He cut her off. "Don't talk. Just carefully look over there and tell me if you recognize who that is."

Josie eyed him skeptically for the moment, but did as he asked. Once she did, she nearly lost her dinner. Both women had been stripped, willingly or not, and both were pleasuring a man standing like a golden statue in the center of an altar. The men who'd come in the cars had formed a tight circle around the center stage and were hooting, cheering and chanting as if they were at a hockey game rather than watching two women service one very large male. Josie ducked back behind the crate with a hand cupped over her mouth.

"Any ideas?" he asked.

"Other than demanding bleach for my eyeballs, no."

It wasn't sex she was watching. It was debauchery. Exploitation. Pornography in living, breathing color.

This wasn't any pagan ritual she'd ever witnessed, that was for sure.

"I've never seen him."

"He's huge," Rick muttered.

She arched a brow, wondering exactly what part of the man Rick was referencing.

"Tall," he clarified. "Broad. I tried not to look at anything else."

"Good policy."

"I think he's demon, from the entry mark, but did you see his eyes?"

She managed a half nod, not willing to lie. She'd only looked for a split second and his eyes were not what she'd noticed first. "Let's get out of here."

For a second, she thought Rick had turned to determine their quickest path to freedom, but instead, he stopped dead. She wondered what he could possibly see from their hiding place, and then realized it wasn't what he'd seen that had made him freeze—but what he heard.

Ruhin. Ruhin.

"What else are they saying?"

Josie tried to listen, tried to use her scant knowledge of Latin to translate the chant. She picked up the words *power, time* and *slave.*

Rick unsheathed the modified Taser he kept beneath his jacket. "Is that him? Or are they calling him?"

Josie shook her head, held up her hand and tried to decipher more while ignoring the enflamed catcalls and feminine moaning and squealing that now accompanied the chant. Clearly, one of the girls onstage no longer had her mouth occupied.

"It's a call, definitely a call."

"Then we should stick around," Rick said.

A shadow dashed in front of them. "Yeah, why don't you?"

Josie ducked behind Rick, but the man caught them both unawares. He kicked the weapon out of Rick's hand, but his concentration on the Taser opened him up for a tackle. Rick pushed him hard against the wall, the grunts and curses loud enough to cause a falter in the chanting and moaning.

Josie spun, unsure what to do. She searched for the Taser,

but the dim light and the stacks of detritus kept her from finding it. Instead, she shoved her hand into her blouse and yanked out the amulet. Could she use it to call Regina? To summon help?

She never got to find out.

Rick heard the cackle of laughter and the thud of a body hitting the floor before he managed to spin around. Josie was on the ground. She didn't stir, didn't move. When the attacker raised a thick slab of wood for a second strike, Rick punched his assailant unconscious, then spun a kick in the direction of the man with the plank. His heel connected with a chin. The wood went flying and the man spun like a top, then crumpled to the floor.

That got the attention of the circle. Even the big guy getting it on with the two women looked up. His eyes glowed an impossibly gleaming black and he shouted something unintelligible to Rick, but sobering to his followers. The women rolled off the altar and cowered as if suddenly aware of their nudity while the men, blinking away confusion, hesitated long enough for him to formulate a plan.

He didn't have a weapon he could use. Except against the giant, he wouldn't fire in here, anyway. These weren't demons. They were humans. Misguided and drugged-up losers who latched on to vice to give their pathetic lives meaning, but humans nonetheless. Mundanes, like him. Like Josie. Luckily, the drugs they'd taken had muddled their brains. By the time they started running toward them, he'd scooped Josie into his arms and barreled out the door.

Because she was unconscious, her weight bore down on him like a stone. He struggled to hold her close and sprint at the same time, heading toward the lights, toward the street, where passing cars might provide some kind of protection from the chasers. Instead, he nearly slammed into the side of a speeding cab that screeched to a halt in front of him.

"Get in!" the driver shouted.

He had only a split second to register Mario's gruff voice before he yanked open the door and threw Josie inside. He spun in time to see the Left Hand supplicants pulling up hard in their tracks.

Mario was pointing a gun through the window. A big gun.

"Get in," the old man repeated.

Rick didn't have to be asked a third time. He dove in beside Josie. Mario's acceleration slammed the door shut. Out of the rearview he watched the group standing dumbly at the curbside. In the background, he caught the eerie glow of the being who'd materialized on the altar. He stood, naked and bold, in the open. He didn't care who saw.

Was it Ruhin himself?

Rick couldn't worry about that now. He turned to Josie, who made a mewling noise as they hit a pothole. Mario cursed, then swung onto the nearest street, putting as much distance as possible between them and the warehouse. Rick flew hard against the glass, then scrambled to Josie, who was still unconscious.

"What the hell happened?" Mario shouted.

Rick slid his fingers onto Josie's neck. Her pulse beat hard and he nearly choked on his sigh of relief.

"Josie? Josie, *por favor,* talk to me."

Her eyelids fluttered but did not open.

"Go to a hospital," Rick ordered. "She might have a concussion."

In what seemed like hours but was more like five minutes, Mario screeched into the parking lot of a brightly lit hospital. Rick bundled Josie into his arms and tore inside. Amid the crowd in the waiting room, he caught sight of a nurse in gray scrubs who met his frantic stare and rushed to him.

"What happened?" she asked.

"Attacked," Rick answered. "Hit on the head, I think. I didn't see it."

"This way," she directed.

Josie was on a gurney in a second, then shunted into a trauma room, where she opened her eyes the minute one of the doctors flashed a light into her face. Rick jostled forward, grabbing her outstretched hand.

"What happened?" she asked Rick.

"You got clocked," Rick replied, forcing a smile. She was awake. Alive. But it was hard to fake happiness when her injury was his fault.

"Don't do it, Rick," she warned.

The nearest doctor looked at him suspiciously.

"Do what?"

"Blame yourself."

"Miss, you need to lie back," the nurse instructed.

Again, Rick was pushed out of the way. He buried his hands in his pockets and listened to Josie answer the doctor's questions and state, for probably one hundred times before they heard her, that she would be fine. When another trauma entered the E.R., the doctors dispersed, leaving only one nurse, who insisted Josie stay for more tests.

"I'm not a criminal, you know," Josie snapped at the nurse. "You can't keep me here."

"No, I can't," the nurse replied, unfazed. "But I'd rather you not show up here again five minutes before I'm set to go home to my kids, all passed out and purple, okay? Do the tests. If you're really fine, you'll be out of here in a few hours."

"Hours?"

The nurse waved her hand and exited the room.

Josie swung her feet off the bed, but nearly swooned as her equilibrium failed to come up with her.

"Oh, goddess," she cursed.

"Let's keep the supernatural out of this," Rick said, catching her by the elbows.

"What happened? And I mean after I got hit," she said.

"Not much," Rick said, filling her in. "He came outside in all his glory."

"So he saw us?" she asked.

Rick nodded.

"Do you think he's Ruhin?"

Rick shrugged, his lips pressed tightly to keep him from answering her question. The past two days, sharing his mission with Josie, allowing her light to reinvigorate his quest, had been a dangerous indulgence. She'd nearly been killed twice now. Enough was enough.

"Don't think it," Josie warned.

"Don't think what?"

"About leaving me behind."

"You're psychic now?"

"I haven't had to be psychic to read your mind up until now," Josie replied tersely. "You're blaming yourself for me getting hurt. You're thinking you're going to take off the minute I go to radiology for the tests the doctor ordered and that this time, you'll hide yourself and cover your tracks so well, I'll never hunt you down. Well, you're wrong. I'll find you. I'll find you by putting myself out there so that Ruhin himself will be able to find *me*. Then you'll have to rescue me, won't you?"

"You wouldn't."

"I don't want to," she said. "I've always had an aversion to women with rescue fantasies. But Rick, I swear on all that is holy in your religion and mine that I'll do whatever it takes to keep you from getting yourself killed."

"And I'm not supposed to do the same for you?" he asked, grabbing her arms with more force than he'd intended. The monitor registering her heartbeat screeched in protest. "You're going to die if you stick with me, Josie. What else has to happen to prove that?"

"Nothing," Josie answered. "I know what I'm doing, what we're doing, is dangerous. But I can't leave you to do this alone. Why do we keep having this same argument?"

"Because you keep almost getting killed!"

Josie had never been so happy to see an orderly in her whole life. The woman walked into the room behind an empty wheelchair, chattering about getting Josie in for tests, oblivious to the fact that she'd just interrupted a serious conversation. If Josie hadn't believed in the goodness of the goddess before that moment, she did now.

She needed the interruption. Because otherwise, she'd have to admit to Rick that she loved him. And that her fear for him had just ratcheted up to unbearable levels.

"We'll finish this when you get back," he said as the nurse helped her into the rolling chair.

"You'll still be here?" she asked.

He cursed. The nurse skewered him with a glare. "Sorry," he said obligingly. "Yeah, Josie. Of course I'll still be here."

As she left him behind, she wondered if this news was good or bad.

Only after she'd gone into the elevator with the orderly did she finally start feeling the pain of all that had happened. Her head hurt. Her shoulders and neck ached and her skin felt coated in dirt and grime. She'd been disgusted by what she'd seen at the warehouse, but not surprised. She had prepared herself for the possibility of tangling with the dark side of humanity, the dark side of magic.

What she'd been wholly unprepared for was the intensity of her feelings for Rick. When she'd first decided to go after him, it had been out of a sense of responsibility. She'd cared about him, and now that she knew about the magical world, she wanted to help him transition as she had into understanding how mundanes and magicals like Lilith and Regina could live harmoniously in the same world. The more she'd discovered about why he'd left and what he'd done while he'd been gone, the more she'd wanted to save him. From the evil, yeah, but also from himself. From the first minute they'd met, she'd recognized a brand of goodness in him that she'd seen in few men before.

She had to admit that while she searched for Rick, she'd fallen in love with who he'd been—responsible, loved, good at his job and caring of the people around him. But now that she'd spent time with him, made love to him, shared his secrets, his fears, his ambitions—she couldn't help loving the man he was now, darkness and all, even more deeply.

So deeply it hurt.

And what would he do if she told him?

She had nothing on which to base any suppositions. She'd never told a man she loved him before.

Never.

"Okay, we're here," the orderly announced as they approached Radiology. "Let's get this done so you can go home."

"I don't know if that's a good thing."

"That hot man you were fighting with in the E.R....he didn't do this to you, did he?" the hospital worker asked shamelessly and with a strong hint of indignation.

"No, but he blames himself."

"Good. Don't trust a man who doesn't take the blame, even when it's not his fault," he replied with a snicker.

"I don't think I've really trusted any man before."

"You're a smart woman," the orderly replied.

"I don't know about that. But damn, I love him like crazy."

"So why do you sound so sad about it?"

15

ON THE WAY HOME from the hospital, Rick and Josie hardly exchanged a word. He sat with her cuddled against his chest, holding an ice pack to the back of her head while Mario drove them home, sensing her silent understanding that they wouldn't discuss what had happened at the warehouse or what would happen as a result until they were alone. Rick hadn't wanted to call Mac in Chicago and hadn't even been sure he'd answer his old cell-phone number. But he'd called him before they left the hospital, and the conversation with his former chief of detectives, while quick, had not been anything like he'd expected.

Mac had seemed genuinely happy to hear from him, even after he'd told him about Josie's injury.

"I know," Mac had said. "Lilith woke up hours ago with the vision. She's alerted Regina."

"Is she on her way?"

"Where are you?"

Rick had given him the address of the apartment Josie had borrowed from her friend. Lilith took the phone at that moment and told Rick to use Josie's necklace after they arrived and Regina would appear shortly thereafter. She'd started to say something else, but Mac came on the line and, after reassuring him that Regina could be trusted, he'd hung up.

Rick had held on to the pay phone longer than necessary, then slung it into the cradle with enough force to garner the attention of a passing nurse. He'd apologized, then hurried back to the exam room so he and Mario could listen to the doctors say that, luckily, Josie only had a mild concussion and that, in addition to routine ice packs and lots of fluids, she simply needed peace and quiet to recover.

The very last thing Rick suspected she'd get once she summoned Regina.

Mario helped them up to the apartment, then promised that he and Iris would be by in the morning to bring them breakfast and check on Josie, no matter how much Rick begged them otherwise. Mario countered his protestations with such a look of blame and fury, Rick gave in. Josie had been hurt on his watch. He really didn't have any reason to keep Josie's friends from making sure he hadn't done worse.

He settled Josie onto the couch and grabbed a bottled water from the refrigerator to hand to her.

"You okay?" he asked sheepishly.

She took a deep breath, then shifted to adjust the position of the ice pack she'd shoved between the back of the couch and her head. "To be honest, I'm more freaked out by what we saw than by what happened to me. What's wrong with those women?"

She grimaced. Rick couldn't resist laughing. Was she more disturbed by the degradation of Dizzy and her companion than by the presence of a very unusual demon?

"Call Regina."

"Rick," she started to argue.

He took her hand and placed it on the center of her chest, right around the location of where the necklace should be. "Call her."

She hesitated, biting her bottom lip for a few seconds, then dug into her shirt and palmed the heart-shaped bloodstone, closed her eyes and spoke Regina's name.

Suddenly, a high-pitched noise filled his ears. A split second of odd ringing later and a woman, dressed entirely in dark purple, materialized in the center of the room. Her mouth tilted into a regal if not haughty grin and memories flooded Rick's mind, no matter how he tried to block the impressions. Just like before, she was here to help, even if he didn't much like her attitude.

"Well, if it isn't the Queen Witch," he snapped.

She ignored him. "Josie, are you all right?"

Josie huffed, clearly annoyed. "It's just a mild concussion. I'll be fine."

Regina St. Lyon spared Rick a cursory glance, then strode to Josie and placed her hand softly on her shoulder. "I promised I'd let you handle the situation yourself, but you've done all you can, I believe. Lilith has been meditating on you for days. She's had flashes of your…activities."

Josie glanced aside and, though he'd only turned on one lamp since their return from the hospital, he was certain she was blushing to the roots of her hair.

"We didn't need monitoring," Rick said.

Regina barely turned in his direction. "Not for most of your activities, no. But had you contacted me before now, perhaps Josie wouldn't have been hurt."

Rick opened his mouth to argue, but Josie beat him to it. "Don't, Regina. Rick feels responsible enough as it is."

"He should."

"No, he shouldn't," Josie countered. "He's only doing what he has to do. And sometimes, there's a price to pay for doing the right thing."

Regina did not seem affected by Josie's argument. "What happened?"

Rick strode forward and put himself between Josie and Regina. He hadn't seen Lilith's sister since the night she'd manipulated the crime scene so Mac and Lilith weren't charged with a double homicide, and her majestic bearing irked him now just as it had then. He knew she was important in the magical world and that her persona likely made her job of protecting witches a whole lot easier, but it still chafed him.

"How much do you know?" Rick asked.

"I know you've left Chicago in search of a particular demon and that you weren't hesitant to kill a few others in the process."

"Old news," Rick said. "How much do you know about what's happened since Josie found me?"

Regina frowned. "Not as much as I'd like. Josie has a very powerful aura. She's managed to block most of her activities from Lilith's visions and as she's probably explained to you, I have no power to track mundanes who do not wish for my help. Once you left your hotel after your explosion, I was unable to find you again until you called Mac."

Rick couldn't help briefly resenting the situation. He'd been motivated to call by Josie's injury, fearing that without intercession by the Guardian of Witches, she might suffer worse next time. And if she hadn't been at the warehouse in the first place, he would have taken on the demonlike being who'd manifested on the altar rather than engaging his minions. But truth be told, he would not have killed the others. And he'd have been outnumbered. He would have lost. Maybe having Josie there hadn't been so bad—saving her meant saving his own ass.

"So now you're here, why?"

She arched a brow. "You called me, remember?"

"Yeah, but Josie seems to think that once you've got me, you aren't going to let me in on this operation."

"My decision will be based entirely on you. Tell me what you know and from that, I'll formulate the next plan of action."

Her calm reply pissed him off. She acted as if he had to obey her orders—as if he was just another minion in her magical realm.

"I don't have to tell you anything," he spat.

His contrary tone didn't ruffle her in the least. "No, you don't. Neither does Josie. But I can help you, which is what you wanted or you wouldn't have called."

"I don't want Josie to get hurt again," Rick insisted.

Regina nodded. "A noble intention and one that I share. And though you may not believe me, Rick, I do not wish for you to be hurt, either. Who have you been seeking…and who, now, is seeking you?"

Rick hesitated. Once he gave up his information, Regina wouldn't need him anymore. Just as easily as she'd appeared out of nowhere, she might have the power to send him off to the Himalayas or Timbuktu or Antarctica. As strongly as he knew that he'd do anything to save Josie from further pain, he also knew that he had to be the one to confront the demon. Not only because of his great-grandmother's prophecy, but because he felt it in his gut. And if there was one thing he'd learned as a cop, it was that his gut was never wrong.

Regina chuckled mirthlessly. "You hesitate even now. If you are trying to figure out how to escape here and leave Josie in my care, know that I will not keep her anywhere against her will. You may be good at hiding, but all the evidence I've gathered tells me you're after one specific demon." She narrowed her eyes, focusing on Josie, who took that moment to determine the shape and temperature of her ice pack.

"And Josie knows who it is, doesn't she?" Regina guessed correctly. "Well, then, even if you disappear on us, she can just track the demon as you have been. That ought to lead her straight to you, shouldn't it? Of course, it will only put her in more danger, but maybe you don't give a damn about that.

Maybe you're so wrapped up in your personal vendetta that you don't care who gets hurt."

"That's not true," Rick said evenly.

"Then prove it. Tell me the name of the demon you seek."

An unseen wind seemed to riffle through Regina's long, dark hair. Her eyes, deep purple and intensely focused, appeared to glow hot and wide. Rick felt a burning in the pit of his stomach, but whether it was from the effects of Regina's obvious fury or his own sickened response to the fact that Josie was now trapped in his nightmare, he wasn't sure.

From her place on the couch, Josie snagged Regina's hand and whispered her name.

The sensation stopped when Regina turned aside.

"I am the Guardian Witch," she insisted to both of them. "These matters are best left to those with the power to stop the evil. You know, now, after the amulet saved you, that the danger I warned you of is not exaggerated. You've nearly died twice. What more proof do you need? Tell me the name of the demon."

Josie flashed Rick a sympathetic look, but obeyed the witch's command and recounted the events of that past two days, leaving out the super-hot lovemaking and, surprisingly, the coven invoking the name of Ruhin. It was as if she knew that he had to be the one to speak the name aloud.

"And despite the fact that you are now the hunted," Regina said to Rick, "you will not abandon your unwise pursuit?"

"No can do, your worship."

She arched a brow. "If you insist on thrusting yourself into my business," she snapped, "the least you can do is understand our hierarchy. I am not royalty, Rick, I'm a Guardian. There are seven of us, each assigned to a continent. Together, we make up the Council of Witches. I am but one of a powerful governing party. As this situation currently only affects my portion of the world, I have not yet alerted the council. But if you force my hand, you'll have more magic working against you than I suspect you want to imagine. My job is to keep witches safe from threats such as the ones you are pursuing. Allow me to complete the task that was assigned to me from birth."

"I'm not a witch," he replied. "You don't have to protect me. Focus on Josie. Get her the hell out of here."

"My taking Josie out of the situation will not stop you," she countered coolly. "But perhaps binding Josie to you will."

His hand fisted. Never in his life had he ached to smash his knuckles into a woman's face before, but her cold, superior expression pushed him closer to the edge than he'd been in weeks. At the same time, he knew he couldn't move so much as a threatening pinkie before she'd blast him with her magical *mojo*. And she knew it, too, though she had the class to simply look at him blankly rather than bait him.

Besides, she wasn't the enemy. Not anymore.

"If you bind Josie to me, she'll die."

"All the better reason for you to abandon this quest."

"All the better reason for you to take Josie somewhere safe and keep her there until I can figure out what Ruhin wants from me."

Regina's eyes widened. "Who? Who is after you?" Her voice echoed with a surprising edge of fear.

"A demon claimed the name was Ruhin," Rick said. "And the group that nearly killed us tonight was chanting his name."

"Do you know who that is?" Josie asked, anxiously.

Despite Regina's lack of an immediate reply, the stunned look in her amethyst eyes spoke volumes. She knew Ruhin, all right. And what she knew wasn't good.

"Yes, I know of him," she said, her mouth curved into a deep frown. "And it looks like you've got your wish, Rick. If Ruhin is the demon you face, then you will do so without my intervention."

REGINA STUMBLED onto the couch beside Josie, who grabbed her elbow, suspecting she was ill. Why else would she lose her balance? The woman was supernaturally strong. She'd get Rick out of this mess. She had to.

"What did you just say?" Josie asked.

Regina took a deep breath, and repeated her cold declaration. "I can't help Rick. And if you stay with him, which I expect you will, I can't help you, either."

"You're the Guardian Witch," Josie insisted. The pit of her stomach seemed to have plunged to her feet. This had to be bad. Really, really bad. Regina wouldn't abandon them for any reason she could think of. "It's your duty to help us."

But even as the claims spilled from Josie's lips, Regina shook her head emphatically.

"You don't understand. This isn't a matter of choice. I cannot help, no matter how much I want to."

Rick snorted and any sign of compassion and concern she'd spied in him earlier had deserted his face. His dark eyes gleamed with disgust. "Isn't this classic? You beg me to stop, and you send Josie that medallion to help protect her while she talks me back to Chicago, and now you say there's nothing you can do about the big bad demon?"

"You're not hearing me," Regina said, her voice taut enough for Josie to realize that her inability to assist them was eating her up inside. "In this quest, I am powerless." She spun in her seat, locking eyes with Rick. "You have to do this. I now see. The premonition your great-grandmother had was correct. You are the one."

Rick arched a doubtful brow. "A minute ago I was public enemy number one to the witching world, and now I'm your only hope? What the hell just happened?"

"This is wrong," Josie muttered, watching the scene unfold in front of her as if she was in a horrible dream. Her head pounded. The painkillers were wearing off while the ice pack was slushy and no longer providing any relief. She threw it onto the coffee table and rounded on Regina, trying not to succumb to her physical exhaustion by losing her temper.

"Just a few days ago, you told me Rick had to stop. You threatened his life if I couldn't convince him to leave the demon-hunting to the experts. Now you want him to risk his life against a demon even you're too afraid to face?"

Regina shot to her feet. "Afraid? Afraid?" Her volume increased with each repetition. "You think that's why I cannot pursue this monster? Without hesitation, I've faced demons and hunters and creatures that are not written about in those books you collect. Fear is not keeping me from doing what needs to be done."

"Why else?"

The atmosphere shifted again in the room and Josie nearly jumped out of her skin when a man in black leather emerged from the shadows with no warning. He looked every inch what she imagined a vampire might look like, without the cloak or fangs. Ebony hair hung like shimmering curtains along the side of a face dark with stubble and centered with eyes as obsidian as the stone he wore around his neck. Hanging by a leather strap, the jewel inside swirled with inky blackness, as if the center were alive.

Josie might have flung herself into Rick's arms if he hadn't grabbed her hand and tugged her behind him before she had a chance.

Rick reached for the gun he'd tucked into his boot, but the stranger put his hand out. "Don't shoot the messenger."

"Who are you?" Rick asked.

"He's mine." Regina's tone was a possessive purr even as her eyes turned hard. "You heard? Did you bring the book?"

He held out a small volume that looked minuscule in his

beefy hands. Neither Josie nor Rick moved to take it, even after Regina folded herself into the man's arms and kissed him passionately.

Josie came out from behind Rick. "Oh. You must be Brock."

With a sigh, Regina unglued herself from the man's chest and made introductions. Brock Aegis, she explained, was her husband, a former witch hunter who'd changed sides and now helped her train the protection squads that had been so rare before the war with Brock's former boss—the very squads Josie had hoped would ride to the rescue and extract Rick from this situation. But with Brock looking as dour and hopeless as Regina, she wondered if any of them would get out this alive.

No. She couldn't allow herself to fall victim to either fear or despair. Not now. Not when Rick needed her. She'd spent a lifetime trying to prove she was tougher than anyone ever gave her credit for, and she wasn't going to prove otherwise when Rick needed her most. To that end, she focused on the good news.

"Lilith didn't tell me you were married," Josie said, tamping down the romantic smile she knew was totally inappropriate under the circumstances.

Regina glanced at the intimidating man behind her, only allowing her expression to remain adoring for an instant, but long enough for Josie to recognize the deep love simmering there.

"It's a new development. Up until very recently, there hasn't been time for romance. We've concentrated on rebuilding the squads, and checking the rise to power of the warlock, who nearly took my sister from me. That's what led me to watch over you, Rick. I had no idea we'd be dealing with Ruhin."

"He's worse than Old Movert," Brock grumbled.

"Who?" Josie asked.

"Ancient witch hunter," Regina replied. "Dead now, thanks to Brock."

"And this Ruhin is worse, how?" Josie asked.

"He's untouchable," Regina said. "Or at least, he will be soon, if you don't stop him."

She directed that to Rick, who'd taken a few steps back and was surveying the scene with a clear mixture of wariness and mistrust.

Josie finally took the book that Brock had offered. She didn't recognize the title, which was in Latin, but easily translatable to read *The Saint's Lament*.

"Saint? As in Catholic saints?" Rick asked.

"Not just Catholics have saints," Regina explained. "When the mayor attacked Lilith and Mac, he had this book on him. I took it. Brock has been examining it for clues."

Josie eyed him curiously. "You read Latin?"

He shrugged. "I was raised on it, along with several other languages. I didn't think it would be much help, but now that Regina has mentioned Ruhin, the context is clear."

Josie was starting to get chills up her spine whenever anyone mentioned the demon's name. "Who is Ruhin?"

Regina looked straight at Rick when she answered. "A demon soul who cannot be stopped by a Wiccan. Not if he's after what I think he's after."

"Which is?" Rick asked.

Brock stepped nearer and Regina took his hand. "Complete and utter control over mundanes everywhere. And only you, Rick Fernandez, can stop him."

16

"SUDDENLY I'M YOUR go-to guy? Why?"

Regina strode forward and Rick held steady, prepared to fight even though he knew he'd likely lose. If the witch with her magic didn't strike him down, her murderous-looking husband would. He might have claimed to be mundane, as their type liked to call nonmagical people like him and Josie, but regular Joes didn't shimmer out of the shadows from nowhere.

When Regina reached for him, Rick reacted, blocking her hand with his grip around her wrist. He felt certain he heard the Brock guy growl, but he didn't move.

Clearly, the man knew his wife could take care of herself.

"May I?" she asked politely, her eyes flicking to his neck.

"You gonna break it?"

"I will exhibit utmost care."

He released her. She ran a cool finger along his neckline, then snagged the gold chain beneath his collar and fished out his crucifix, cradling the gold cross gingerly atop her fingers.

"This is why you must take on this task," she said. "A Wiccan cannot stop Ruhin if he's after what he's been seeking for centuries. We're pagan. Our gods and goddesses do not rule over the weapon he desires."

Rick flicked a glance at the book in Josie's hand. "What weapon is that?"

"A relic," Brock replied. "The hand of St. Augustina."

The color drained from Josie's face, but with Regina still cradling his crucifix in her palm, he thought it better not to make any sharp moves toward her. Josie lowered herself onto the couch again. "A hand?"

Gingerly, he removed the gold pendant from Regina's grip and stepped aside, joining Josie near the couch. He'd grown up on tales of relics. He had an aunt who claimed to have a sliver from the canoe of Rodrigo and Juan de Hoyos, the Cuban fishermen who were reportedly witnesses to a vision of the Virgin Mary commonly known as *Caridad del Cobre*. His aunt had claimed the bit of wood, encased in a series of glass boxes within glass boxes, had been taken from Batista's estate during the revolution and had healed her grandmother of cancer. No amount of scientific evidence to the contrary would convince her—or anyone else in the family—of its lack of authenticity. Not even when her husband had dropped dead of a heart attack two feet from the altar in their living room where she kept the religious knickknack.

"How do you know about this hand, then? And about Ruhin?"

Brock cleared his throat. "I come from a long line of witch hunters, descended from the most pious men of Spain."

"Then why don't you fight him?" Josie challenged, her words a mixture of bitterness and fear.

Brock shook his head. "Piety and faith are two different things, Josie. I'm sorry, but I was never raised to believe in anything except killing witches. But I know my church history. It was part of the training, particularly when the history interlocked with magical phenomena. Which it does. More often than many people think."

"Then tell me who this St. Augustina is, because I've never heard of her," Rick demanded. Thirteen years of Catholic school and a lifetime with his own family—both pious *and* faithful—gave him a pretty good knowledge of those people who'd been singled out as saints. "There's a St. Augustine, but I don't remember an Augustina."

"She's very little known," Brock answered gruffly. "At least, in the catechisms. In books like that one, probably not so much."

Josie flipped to the back and then the front, probably for an index, which unfortunately didn't exist. Rick watched her sigh, then turn to page one and run her fingers down the text, searching for the name, he was certain.

"Why the low profile?" Rick asked.

Brock tilted his head toward the couch. While Regina slipped into the spot beside Josie, Rick remained standing. Brock took a seat on a chair across from them all.

"Ruhin, if my memory serves, was a problem previously, though he's apparently kept out of the spotlight. He killed several hunters while pursuing a witch who had a lead on the hand of St. Augustina."

"It's missing?" Rick asked.

Brock shook his head. "Hidden. Legend says that—"

"*Tantum humanus reperio, tantum fidelis tactus,*" Josie said, her voice peaking with excitement. She spun around, her finger pressed to a passage that had been marked with a symbol of a scarlet-red crescent. "I've seen that symbol. That's how Lilith figured out that the mayor was a warlock."

Regina glanced at the symbol and nodded. "Yes, that's the sign of a powerful sect of warlocks who set up shop in Italy, the cradle of Roman Catholicism. You can't have a demon without a warlock."

Again, Rick ran through the knowledge he'd taken into his mind. Demons were made when warlocks died. Warlocks, the male children of a female witch and a particularly sociopathic mundane male, stole the skills of witches to gain power, usually killing them in the process. Warlocks, however, could be killed by conventional means, whereas demons were heartier. The shadow soul that had tried to take Rick back in Chicago had been old and powerful. Ruhin must have started out as a warlock, then become a demon. But the mayor had been a warlock, so Rick didn't understand how this progression was possible.

Regina must have seen the confusion on his face.

"If a demon is powerful when it is killed," Regina explained, her voice softening even as her eyes narrowed on Rick, "then its soul descends only to the middle realm."

Brock suddenly became interested in the lightening sky outside the apartment. Rick watched the way the big man moved and realized that the jerkiness in his gait meant the topic had listed into stormy territory.

"The middle realm?" Josie asked.

"It's like purgatory," Rick explained, "before purgatory became politically incorrect."

Josie drew her hands on either side of her face as if squeezing her skull would keep the madness of all this horrible knowledge from exploding in it.

"That's not exactly correct, but it's close," Regina conceded. "Souls trapped in the middle realm can return to earth, though it takes very powerful magic to pull it off."

The Guardian Witch glanced over her shoulder at her husband. After a few seconds, he turned and gave her a very small, very private and, clearly, very meaningful smile. Whatever tension existed between the two instantly lifted and Regina continued her explanation with greater urgency. "If the soul of a warlock returns, it can find the body of a soulless human and invade it. That's what demons are. At some point, Ruhin must have taken over the body of another warlock, like the mayor, thus doubling his power. He's likely gone back and forth between creatures for centuries, amassing a store of evil power that is unmatched by our standards."

As Josie mulled over the information, her grip on the book loosened. Rick leaned across and took it, doing his best to translate the Latin, though it had been years since he'd taken Introduction to Dead Languages in college. He recognized the name of St. Augustina beside the crescent symbol and spotted the reference to her hand and then the phrase, printed in bold script, that Josie had read aloud.

"Only a human can find," he translated.

"Only the faithful can touch," Brock added. "The hand is a source of great power over mundanes."

"The power of God?" Rick asked.

Brock shook his head. "Not according to what I was taught. The hunters believed the hand was cut off by the demon—or the warlock—when he became incensed that she wouldn't give in to his temptation. She held strong to her faith and recovered from her maiming. She grew a new hand. Died with it, too, which is why the relic was written off by the church as not authentic. How could the hand be hers when she had two not only after her burial, but years later when her body was exhumed for examination? That's why you haven't learned of this story in your catechism.

"However, the demon who took the hand imbued it with all the magic this beast had accumulated over time. The hand is said to be able to sway the will of all mundanes. I have no idea if that's true, but the last time it was reportedly spotted, an entire expedition of Spanish explorers were massacred, re-portedly, by each other. A diary found at the scene spoke of a hooded stranger carrying a severed hand."

"When was this?"

Brock returned to the center of the room. "About five hundred years ago in Mexico."

"So Ruhin was the one who took Augustina's hand?" Josie asked. Having taken back the book, she was reading earnestly, her eyes close to the page, her fingers underscoring every line.

Brock frowned. "We don't know. If he was, he somehow lost it. Maybe he had the knowledge when he was a warlock and when he died and was reborn as a demon, he lost it. He returned to the living realm and has been searching for it ever since. That's all speculation. The last witch who battled him did so in Italy in the eighteenth century."

"Did she win?" Josie asked.

"My guess is that she got rid of him but that again, he wasn't destroyed. She told the hunters who caught up to her, and who murdered her soon after, that he was seeking the hand of St. Augustina."

"Maybe he just wanted to marry her?" Rick offered, an underlying dark humor lacing his voice.

"That's not funny," Regina snapped.

Rick shrugged. She was right. None of this was the least bit humorous. But despite the wild improbability of the theory, certain aspects did make sense. He'd been tracking the movements of the former Chicago mayor's closest advisors and all but one had ended up being connected to the magical world. Each had connections to demons who had formed nests and sent their workers out on a long journeys to retrieve…something. Luckily for him, most hives had only four or five beasties and they only returned to the fold on the full moon. That gave him time to track them down and destroy them, one by one.

"The mayor had connections to demon nests in Chicago, Detroit, Pittsburgh and New York," he informed them, realizing that while he had knowledgeable people in his midst, he needed to exploit their expertise. "I never heard the name Ruhin until this morning."

Regina pursed her generous lips. "Ruhin is an old demon. He would likely hide his connections."

"He tried to take over Rick," Josie said.

Regina and Brock exchanged dark glances.

"Trying to invade a human? A live human?" Brock asked. "Why?"

Regina nodded. "Because he can't touch the hand as a warlock or a demon. He needs the body of a faithful human to obtain what he so desires. It makes perfect sense."

"That's good to know," Rick said, sarcasm dripping from his tone. "As long as it all makes sense, we're good to go."

Regina stepped closer to Rick, eyeing him with a mixture of concern and something else—envy perhaps? "This is likely more than you bargained for, Rick. If you want to back out and leave the hunting to us, the time to say so is now."

Rick turned, purposefully avoiding Josie's pleading gaze. "No one has been able to destroy him before now?"

Regina instinctively touched the amethyst amulet she wore around her neck, as if for strength. "I suspect that his soul is tied to the hand, since it is likely his magic that created it. As long as it exists, his soul will not descend to the lowest realm, from where it cannot return, until the hand of St. Augustina is destroyed. And to do that, we need you."

So he had to track down a severed hand if he was ever to be free of Ruhin's specter. He'd seen enough weird shit over the past six months to believe that the hand not only existed, but that it possessed the power Regina and Brock believed it did.

"I'll do it, but I'm doing it alone."

"Like hell you will," Josie protested.

The time for playing nice was over. He grabbed Josie by the arm and squeezed hard. He watched pain glaze her eyes, but she pressed her lips tightly together, refusing to surrender. She was braver than he'd ever imagined, he'd give her that. But in this case, brave could get her dead.

"Hell is precisely where I'm going," Rick said. "And I'm not taking you with me."

"I'm Wiccan. I don't believe in hell."

"Then I'll believe enough for both of us."

17

Josie didn't want to understand more about Rick's beliefs. She knew enough to respect them, but under the stress of the new information about the limitations of magic in this circumstance, she only wanted to desperately cling to her own. *An ye harm none, do as ye will.*

But how could they stop Ruhin without hurting someone? Especially Rick.

"How do we find this hand?" she asked.

Rick took the ice pack away from her, went into the kitchen, dumped the icy water into the sink and refilled it with cubes from the freezer. With several whacks that made all of them flinch, he crushed the ice then returned the pack to her.

She didn't even have the nerve to say thank you. He was seething, overloading with all they'd learned. She couldn't blame him. Just when he'd decided to share some of the responsibility of this hunt with Regina, she'd told them there was nothing she could do to help.

"*We* don't find the hand," Rick said. "I'll do it. You've done all you can. Now, you," he said, pointing a finger at Regina, "get her the hell out of here. She's Wiccan. She can't help any more than you can. For this, I'm on my own."

"I'm human," Josie argued. "And I'm faithful. Maybe not to Roman Catholicism, but to Wicca. I have every qualification you have."

"Josie," Rick said, his voice full of dire warning.

She stood up, no matter how woozy it made her feel. She jammed her hands onto her hips and matched his stubborn stance, glare for glare.

"I think this is our cue to leave," Brock said from behind them.

Josie didn't bother to turn around. She fought to remain still even when Regina placed her hand on her shoulder and whispered into her ear.

"Take time to heal," she instructed. "And use the amulet to call me again if you so wish. I will leave the book."

She placed it on the coffee table and a second later the room was less two people.

"You can't fight me on this," Rick said once Regina and Brock were gone.

"I can fight you on anything worth fighting for," she countered. "I won't leave you to deal with this alone. So I got bumped on the head? So what? I'm alive because of you."

Rick's jaw tightened and the veins in his neck were so visible that she knew he was doing everything he could to contain his temper. Finally, he spun around and moved as if to slam his fist into the wall. She screamed for him to stop and he pulled back, his knuckles inches from certain damage. She took a chance, clutching his shoulders and easing him away.

"That's not what happened," Rick said.

"What do you mean?"

"I didn't save your life. You saved mine. If you hadn't gotten hurt, if you hadn't needed me, I would have taken that demon and all his followers on."

"He could have been Ruhin," she said with a gasp.

He nodded. "I wasn't ready to fight him, but I would have. And I might have died, charging in with no plan, no backup. I'm a better cop than that."

"But you did have backup. I'm sorry I had to be knocked

unconscious for you to see that," she said, a quiver of humor in her voice.

He yanked her into his arms and held her so tightly she thought she might pass out again. Instead, she relaxed, curling her head just beneath his shoulder and pressing her ear against his chest so that she could hear the rapid pounding of his heart.

"Rick, don't be afraid for me," she said.

"You're asking the impossible. How can I not be afraid for you when I—"

If she wasn't mistaken, his heart actually skipped a beat. She pulled away. "You what?"

"I love you," Rick said.

His declaration was short and sweet, though there was nothing short or sweet about his delivery. Instead, the words were drawn out by the sheer desperation of his bitter confession.

He loved her. But from the tortured look in his eyes, he did not want to.

She took a moment to swallow, to try and come up with what to say in response. Because while she wanted nothing more than to return the sentiment, to confess the deep bond she'd felt with him since the moment they met, she knew that succumbing to the impulse would do more harm than good. To both of them.

"You don't sound happy about it," she said, the corners of her mouth quirking into a forced smile. She attempted to slide out of his embrace, but he held her steady for a minute, until she stared at him with such immovable resolve, he had no choice but to let her go.

"I'm not," he said. "How can I be when loving you puts you in danger?"

"Well, you could just try to look on the bright side," she replied.

He laughed, in spite of the angst playing in his expression. "I've never been a very optimistic person."

"Are you sure? Because the Rick I used to know had a great sense of fun. He was secure in who he was and what he wanted from life. Secure enough to let into his heart, even just a little bit, a woman who represented everything he wasn't. That woman would be me, by the way, in case you were wondering."

She pressed the ice pack to the back of her head again, less out of necessity and more to dull the ache that seemed to be taking over her entire body.

"I know it's you, Josie. It's always been you. From the moment we met, I knew you were different and I don't mean because you have a juvenile record or because you're Wiccan. It's just…you. When you wandered in to the police station looking for Lilith that day, I was at the perfect place to want a relationship. Something long-term. Something permanent. But then just a few days later, everything changed. Everything except how I feel about you. I've been trying to deny it since you came back into my life, but seeing you last night on the floor of that warehouse, carrying you into that hospital, made me realize that no matter how I've changed over the past six months, my feelings for you are the same."

"You couldn't have loved me then," she argued, though she wasn't exactly sure why. It wasn't every day that a man professed his love for her. In fact, this was the first time in Josie's life that any man ever had—including her father, a man who should have loved her if for no other reason than because she existed. "We'd only known each other for a few days."

"I loved you from the moment I saw you."

She drew her hand to her mouth. This was too much. Too much. More than she expected and, yet, less than she deserved.

She wiped her eyes. "I'm not clairvoyant, but I'm pretty sure there's a 'but' coming in a few seconds."

"Telling a woman you love her implies a promise,

doesn't it? A promise that you'll always be together. That you have this fabulous future planned for her. I can't make those promises."

"I've never asked you to," she replied.

"You deserve promises, Josie. Promises that are kept. And you deserve a future."

"Then why are you telling me all this?" she asked. He was right, of course. But that didn't make her riotous emotions any easier to wrangle. She ached to leap into his arms, bathe his face in kisses, declare her love for him and make love to him until he forgot why telling her that he loved her wasn't a moment of wonder and delight. Instead, she crossed her arms tightly and waited for his answer to her defiant question.

"Because even when this is all over," he said, clutching her above the elbows, "I don't know what's going to happen. I've never been in such an uncertain place before. Living in the moment is the only way to survive. I learned that from you."

She couldn't help but laugh, though the bitter bite in the sound made him release her.

"That's about the only lesson my mother ever taught me that was worth anything. So for the moment, you can love me. As long as there are no promises or expectations."

She managed to keep her voice soft and touched his cheek, not trusting herself to do anything more in case she fell apart, which she refused to do, even as disappointment flooded through her. Rick needed to see her as strong and determined and resourceful. Because she was all those things. Normally. Right now, she felt nothing but.

"I'm going to take a shower," she said. "Then I should get that rest the doctor recommended. In the morning, we can start thinking about exactly how to track down that relic and—"

His face was stony, his mouth set and his eyes devoid of any emotion. "Don't worry about tomorrow." His eyes flicked to the smaller bedroom, where Josie suddenly guessed he'd be spending the night. "If you need anything, just give a shout."

She managed a nod before retreating to the larger bedroom. She shut the door behind her, ignoring the pain in her neck as she went through the motions of preparing for a shower. She stripped off her clothes. Grabbed fresh pajamas from her suitcase. Turned on the water to as hot as she could stand. Once she was enclosed in the glass stall, however, she lost all semblance of control. Memories of making love with Rick in this very same space hit her harder than any two-by-four. Sobs racked her body and tears sluiced down her face with the same force of the water from the showerhead. He loved her, but he didn't love her enough. She had no idea what she wanted from him, but she knew she deserved more than he'd offered. Knew it to the depth of her soul.

He'd put parameters on his love. He'd only love her for now, in the moment, as if this were some sort of triumph. Well, Josie didn't want to be loved only in the here and now. She'd waited long enough, had been through more than her fair share of bad relationships, to know that when she finally had a man love her, she wanted the whole shebang.

After crying herself dry of tears, she gingerly washed, soaping up with the same foam Rick had used to pleasure her body only a few days before, then tried to banish those memories from her thoughts while she rinsed. She toweled, combed and braided her hair, donned her comfortable sleepwear and exited the bathroom to find a fresh glass of water, her painkillers and an ice pack beside her bed.

She glanced at the door. He'd come inside, but had obviously left quickly and once again closed the door. She tried not to read anything more into his thoughtfulness. He loved her, after all. He just didn't love her enough.

After taking her pain pills, she doused the lights and moved to the window. A bracing chill emanated off the glass, making her hug herself for warmth. The glow from the red and pink lights of the Valentine's Day decorations across the alley mocked her, so she drew the shade and got into bed, propping the pillows so she could rest the ice pack behind her head.

She shut her eyes, exhausted, and waited for the medication to kick in. A creak near the door caught her attention, but the quick twist of her head made her wince. In the light beaming in from the beneath the door, she could see that Rick was standing just on the other side.

"Josie? Are you okay?"

She prayed he wouldn't open the door as she said, "I'm fine. Just tired."

"I'll come in and check on you in a little while," he replied.

"You don't have to," she assured him. "I just need to sleep."

Despite her concussion, the doctor hadn't given them any special instructions regarding her care beyond the painkillers and orders of rest. Rick didn't need to check on her and at the moment, the last thing she wanted was him near her bed. Not when her thoughts and feelings were so conflicted and confused.

He didn't reply, but she saw his shadow retreat from her room. The light in the living room remained on and after about ten or fifteen minutes, she thought she heard the sound of the laptop powering up. She removed the ice pack and settled into the pillows, turning away from the door. If he wanted to stay up all night and research the new information about St. Augustina, that was his business.

If she wanted to stay up all night and worry about what she'd say to him in the morning, that was hers.

18

RICK HAD ENDURED many a chewing out by his mother over his lifetime. The time he'd snuck out in the middle of the night to throw rotten oranges at passing cars. The time he'd asked Mary Jane Johnson to the junior high prom instead of Selena Del Diego, whose parents had been friends of the family for years. The time he'd thought that hiding a *Playboy* in the bottom of his underwear drawer was a good idea when his mother was still doing his laundry.

But none compared to the ten-minute tirade his mother had unleashed on him this morning. Well, after being out of contact with his family for six months, he could hardly have expected any less.

"Where are you?"

Finally, his father's voice, calm and measured. Since his heart attack at a young age, Rogelio Fernandez had lived well into his sixties by knowing how to stem the tide of his Latin temperament, something Estela Fernandez, his wife, had never been the least bit interested in doing.

"I think I'd better not tell you, *papa.*"

"You're in danger, then," his father concluded.

"I don't want to talk about my situation," he replied. The less his parents knew, the better. If this demon was truly after him, it wasn't that much of a leap to think the creature might hunt down his parents to discover his location. He could only hope that a house that always had a holy water dispenser near the front door and a statue of the blessed virgin in the front yard would keep any otherworldly beings at bay. "I just…I just wanted to call."

"Six months since we last spoke to you, *hijo*. Did you really think you'd get away with making us worry and not get an earful from your mother? She cried every night like *una hiena*. She waits by the phone every night, hoping that friend of yours will call us and tell us she's found you."

Rick's throat tightened. "Josie's been calling you?"

"Every week," his father replied quickly. "Is she with you?"

"Yes," Rick said, sparing a glance to the door that had remained shut all night, the door he'd pressed his ear to every hour on the hour, listening for any sound that Josie was okay, not daring to open it. She'd made it clear she didn't want him in the room with her last night and despite what he'd admitted to her, he'd kept out. He'd heard her get up this morning and the relief of knowing she was at least physically okay had relieved his mind enough to start thinking about more than just demons and warlocks and loving a woman he couldn't logically commit to. He'd thought about his family and how he'd likely worried them to death by keeping out of contact for so long.

His father repeated the news of Josie's presence to his mother, who seemed to take the information with reinvigorated emotion.

"Mom doesn't like Josie," Rick concluded from the sound of the wailing on the other end of the line.

"Are you *loco?* She's never met her, but she loves her like a daughter. She's been worried about her, too."

Rick frowned. "She doesn't know her."

"She knows that the woman cares enough about you to not only go looking for you, but to call your family and keep them from worrying all alone."

Rick sheepishly turned his back to Josie's bedroom door. "She's very thoughtful," he conceded.

His father was no longer listening. His mother had flown into another rage and was demanding the phone, which his father was trying to keep away from her. Rick chuckled silently, imagining the scene. His father was strong and formidable, but like most Cuban men with more than a lick of sense, he deferred to his wife in most situations. This, however, was not one of those times. Rogelio's voice lowered to James-Earl-Jones-as-Darth-Vader in tone and volume and commanded his wife to be quiet.

Then, he calmly asked Rick, "Your mother wants to know if you are wearing your crucifix."

Instinctively, Rick's hand pressed against the cross-shaped indentation beneath his T-shirt. "I haven't taken it off since you gave it to me."

His father related the news. His mother, now talking in rapid Spanish with a pitch rising to levels Rick suspected soon only dogs would hear, said a few words that traveled over the phone lines. Words like *bisabuela*. And *advertencia*. Warning.

"What's *mami* talking about?" he asked.

"I don't know," his father replied wearily. "Something about your great-grandmother, who gave you the crucifix all those years ago."

Rick's chest tightened even as he grabbed the necklace through his shirt. "You and *mami* gave the necklace to me when I finished the police academy."

"Your mother had been saving it since you were six. Her grandmother gave it to you when we went to Cuba, remember? Shortly before she died? She said it would protect you and that your mother should save it until you were a man. She traveled all the way to the village in Pinar del Río to find this priest who was underground there, just to have him bless it. No other priest would do."

Rick dropped down onto the couch, still clutching the chain and cross beneath the shirt. He'd never thought much about his necklace, but at the same time, he never took it off. He considered it more than just a sign of his religion, but as a good-luck charm. As a beat cop he'd been in a lot of scrapes that had turned his way. At the time, he'd always imagined perhaps the gold had protected him, even when wearing it might have been against regulations. It was one of the few rules he ever broke, but he was careful to keep the religious symbol out of sight.

Even that night when the demon soul had first attacked him, Rick had felt the fire of the gold burning against his flesh. He hadn't thought, until this moment, that the religious symbol blessed by a renegade priest in communist Cuba might have helped him escape the demon's invasion.

"*Papa,* put *mami* on the phone," he insisted.

"Son, she's hysterical. Call us back——"

"*Papa, por favor.* I need to ask her something. *Es muy importante.*"

In the time it took for his father to calm his mother down, Josie emerged from the bedroom looking healed, but tired. Her head injury had clearly taken its toll. Or else, what he'd told her so shortly before bedtime had affected her as it had him. He'd hardly slept a wink. She didn't look like she'd done much better.

When his mother finally came back on the line, Rick motioned for Josie to come closer. He had to stop shutting her out. He knew if he did, he'd lose her for good, and for the first time since he'd admitted how he felt about her, he realized he'd never recover if that happened.

"*Mami,* tell me about the crucifix."

Josie looked at him quizzically, so he pressed the speakerphone option on the cell phone and placed it on the table in front of the couch, beckoning Josie to join him. She did but, not surprisingly, sat a good foot away from him.

"What?"

"I have you on speakerphone, *mami*. Josie is here."

Rick had to endure a few minutes of his mother complaining to Josie about what a terrible and cruel son she had that he didn't call her for six months, but Josie managed to pacify her in record time. Rick arched a shocked eyebrow at her, but she merely smiled confidently. He'd never seen anyone handle his mother with such finesse except, maybe, his older sister, who was unmatched when it came to talking her way into her mother's good graces. Maybe Josie had more in common with his family than he'd anticipated.

"*Mami*, please. It's important that you tell me what *bis-abuela* said about the necklace."

"People thought she was crazy, you know," his mother explained. "She was nearly blind since birth, but she saw things others could not. When we went to visit her before she died, she touched you and had a vision."

Rick gaped. He had no idea that his mother knew. He'd never told anyone what his great-grandmother had told him a few days later in a quiet corner of her garden while they picked sugarcane to suck on in the hot Caribbean sun.

"I didn't know she told you," he admitted.

His mother quieted. "What did she tell you?"

"You first," Rick countered, not wanting to worry his mother if he didn't need to. The woman was already just a few heartbeats away from a panic attack.

"Just that you would one day do a very great thing, but that you would need something for protection. That's when she set out to Pinar del Río. She took your father with her. When she came back, she gave me the crucifix and told me that once you were a man, you had to wear it every day. That it would protect you. When you joined the police academy, I knew that it was the time. Why are you asking me all these questions all of a sudden? Is this why you left Chicago without a word? Are you doing something dangerous? Is that what she saw?"

Rick glanced at Josie and, though she hesitated, she slid her hand on top of his and gave him a little nod.

"Yes. But with Josie's help, I think it'll be over soon. Why did your *abuela* have to go so far away to find a priest?"

"*Yo no se.* There was a priest just outside of Havana who was much closer. But it had to be Father Augustino."

Josie and Rick both reacted with, "Augustino?"

"*Si,* Augustino Marquez de los Rios. He was from Spain, but he came to Cuba after the revolution to keep the faith alive under communist rule. Your great-grandmother adored him, even though as far as I know, she only met him that one time."

Rick drew his hands through his hair. Either this bit of news made no sense at all, or it made all the sense in the world.

"This priest, was he old?"

His mother covered the phone, but though muffled, they could hear her asking Rogelio what he knew about Father Augustino.

"No," she replied. "Your father said he was very young. Maybe thirty."

"Which means he's now in his fifties. Is he still in Cuba?"

Again, she asked his father, but neither one knew the answer. Once their great-grandmother had died, they'd worked to move the remainder of the family to the United States. Their ties with the Caribbean island of their heritage had dropped dramatically.

"Ricardo," his mother said, eliciting a laugh from Josie, who'd never heard him called by his proper name. "What is this all about?"

Rick thought carefully, knowing he had to give his mother an answer that wouldn't send her into another apoplectic fit.

"It's about faith, *mami.* It's about doing the right thing.

That's all, really. There's nothing for you and *papa* to worry about, okay? I'll call you soon."

His mother hummed, as if not convinced. "Josie, you are staying with him?"

"Yes, ma'am. I'm not leaving his side."

"Esta bien," his mother answered, and after a series of goodbyes and warnings and admonitions to call back the next day, Rick hung up the phone.

Silence filled the room for a long moment, during which time Josie took her hand away from his. "This can't be a co-incidence, Rick. None of this."

He shook his head, finding it hard to believe that every detail of this interaction with an evil demon had been prede-termined for so long. He could accept that his great-grand-mother had the clairvoyance to see that he'd battle some great evil later in life, but not that she'd known specifically who it was—or at the very least, specifically who he'd need to find in order to win.

"How good are you at finding Catholic priests?" he asked Josie, a grin tugging at the corners of his mouth. Maybe he did need her after all, because while he was a former police officer, her skills at seeking out someone who didn't want to be found surpassed his by leaps and bounds.

Her smile was a ray of sunshine on an otherwise cloudy day. "I have no idea, but I guess we're about to find out."

19

IN HER WILDEST DREAMS, Josie never would have guessed that
her search for the Cuban priest who had blessed Rick's cross
on the insistence of his clairvoyant great-grandmother would
lead them back to Chicago. But through a combination of his
sleuthing skills and her ability to insinuate herself into just
about any situation and extract the information she needed,
she and Rick walked into a community center on the south
side of the city with a clear picture of who they were seeking.

They found him in the center of a group of rambunctious
children playing a rather raucous game of musical chairs to
the strains of Celia Cruz.

Josie thought the building looked a little run-down, but the
joy in the place overflowed, despite the peeling paint and
mismatched ceiling tiles. The unmistakable scent of roasting
chicken wafted in from a door to their left, and a gaggle of
Hispanic women chatted in Spanish as they set up several long
tables with paper napkins, cups and plates. Clearly, there was
some sort of event going on and Father Augustino, if he was
indeed the salt-and-pepper-haired man racing an eight-year-
old to a folding chair when the salsa song stopped mid-beat,
was in the middle of the action.

Not surprisingly, the child beat him to the chair. The crowd
erupted into laughter and applause and Father Augustino gave
a bow, though he paused in the down position with his hands

on his knees for a few seconds to catch his breath. Josie couldn't help but smile. For a man who was tied, possibly without his knowledge, to a centuries-old demon, he had an incredible sense of fun.

When he scooted out of the way so the game could restart, his gaze made contact with Rick's. Josie watched the exchange with her heart in her throat, though it dropped back into place when the priest glanced at the crucifix Rick now wore on the outside of his shirt, gasped in surprise, then nodded in peaceful complacency. He motioned them further inside, pointing to a door in the back that led to a cramped office overflowing with what looked like prizes for an upcoming raffle.

"I knew you'd come someday," the priest said, his Cuban accent thick and melodious.

"You know who I am?" Rick asked, positioning himself by the door.

Josie, on the other hand, decided to sit. She'd touched the necklace that Regina had given her and it had given off absolutely no warning signals. It was no coincidence to her that both she and Rick wore amulets associated with their own faiths, just as it was no accident that the priest they sought tended a flock less than twenty minutes by train from Rick's apartment.

"Ricardo Fernandez," the priest replied, scooting a box of party hats off his chair and sitting down, folding his fingers on his chest in a steeple. "But this lovely lady, I'm afraid, I do not know."

Josie leaned forward and extended her hand. "Josie Vargas, um, Father? I'm not sure what I should call you."

The priest glanced at her pentagram earrings and bloodstone necklace. "You are not of the faith?"

"Not your faith," Josie said confidently.

The priest gave an uncertain nod and then covered his momentary lapse with a smile that made his light brown eyes twinkle. "Everyone here calls me Father Tino. You may do the same. I apologize for my judgmental attitude. For many years, I've been wary of those who do not follow the same path as I."

"Can't blame you, considering what you must know," Josie replied.

His face grew stony. "I'm afraid I cannot say precisely what I know until I determine why you are here."

"You acted as if you were expecting me," Rick said, his shoulder propped against the doorjamb.

"You, yes," the priest replied. "On the day your great-grandmother came to see me, twenty some-odd years ago, she told me of her vision. I would not have believed such a thing, but she was very convincing. She had me bless the crucifix you are wearing around your neck, and believed that only a blessing from me would protect you. I had no idea who she was or what she was talking about, you see. I was a Spanish priest smuggled into Cuba to minister to the poor. But she knew me, knew of my family legacy, knew things she couldn't possibly have known by any conventional means. I listened to her. She told me your name. She told me that someday, you would finish the work of my family."

Josie covered a gasp with her hand.

"*Sí, señorita.* The saint whose relic you seek was a distant cousin. In every generation, there has been a man or a woman of vocation who has watched over her legacy. Why? We were never sure, until your great-grandmother told me."

"And you didn't think she was crazy?" Rick asked, skeptically.

The priest chuckled. "I suppose I should have, but then again, here you are, wearing the crucifix I blessed and, I suspect, on the trail of something only I can give you. But I'm not sure yet if I should."

"Then let us convince you," Josie said, catching Rick's eye and gesturing toward the chair beside hers.

Rick hesitated, but after receiving permission from the priest to lock the door, he sat down. He started talking and didn't stop for nearly half an hour, recounting everything that had happened since the mayor's death six months ago. The priest listened as intently as if he were hearing confession, or so Josie guessed. He leaned forward, his head tilted, his hands folded as if in prayer and his eyes closed, as if it took every ounce of his concentration to understand the full breadth of what Rick was saying.

"So you believe this evil entity is after the hand of St. Augustina?" he asked at the end of the tale.

"He has been for centuries," Rick replied.

Josie finally had something to add to the conversation. "After we found out that you've been living in Chicago for the past five years, we came back. In my shop, I have a rather extensive collection of books on the occult. We finally found information about St. Augustina that referenced Ruhin, just as we'd been told. He made the relic. He put magical properties into it that would have given him sway over mundanes, humans, to do his bidding. But St. Augustina, with her faith, took back the hand and banished the demon to the middle realm."

The priest eyed Rick questioningly.

"It's like purgatory," Rick explained.

"Only not a permanent place of residence to powerful magical beings," she explained further. "There are ways to escape and clearly, Ruhin has. His soul doesn't even descend anymore. He has to be banished to the lower realm where he cannot return. We believe," Josie said, looking at Rick, "that St. Augustina may have known this. She protected the relic by ensuring that only a human can find it and only a faithful person can touch it—and only someone who wants to destroy Ruhin would even go looking for it."

Father Tino pursed his lips. "Except this Ruhin, who has been looking for it for a very long time."

"But he is not human," Josie said. "He can't find it."

Rick added, "That's why it's so scary that he seems able to transfer from body to body now without the human being near death. If not for this cross, he might have invaded me. If he indeed was inside the man we confronted in New York, then he's able to possess someone young and strong. If he was dying, he certainly didn't look it."

"In other words," Josie clarified, "if he's managed to take a human body that isn't entirely sustained by the demon force, he might be one step closer to possessing the hand."

The priest frowned. "But he cannot enter the body of a faithful person, yes? That is why you were able to resist him?"

Rick swiped his hand over the crucifix. "I can only assume as much. We just don't know."

"But you can find out," the priest said hopefully.

"How?" Josie asked.

"Ask him," the priest said.

Rick and Josie exchanged confused looks.

Father Tino stood. They did the same.

"One thing I have learned from my many years in the priesthood is that there is a time for hiding and a time for confrontation. I believe the time has come for the legacy of St. Augustina to play out. We simply have to determine the place."

"But if we lead him to the hand, he could take it. Become more powerful than he's been in centuries."

"Or you could finally destroy him," the priest said calmly. "Either way, the time has come to finish this, or else, you would not be here."

RICK STOOD in the darkened corner of the mausoleum and watched Josie unpack. She placed item after item on top of the marble altar, every so often glancing at the religious statue behind her as if worried that the droll little cherub didn't approve of her using holy ground for her pagan ritual. Truth was, she did not approve, either. She'd protested vehemently when Father Tino had made the suggestion and only after he assured her that she had explicit permission from him did she agree to comply.

"I have a really creepy feeling about all this," she said, placing the final candle in the fifth corner of the pentagram she'd drawn on the floor around the altar in chalk.

"I know you do," Rick said, "but Father Tino believes this is the only way. And he said we have to do this together."

She arched a skeptical brow at him. "And you need his approval?"

Rick flicked on his flashlight and continued his search around the inside of the mausoleum. Father Tino had directed them to this small marble building in the corner of the cemetery bordered by his parish. He'd implied that the hand of St. Augustina was hidden here. Rick had asked the priest to simply turn it over, but the man had declared that if and when Rick needed it, he'd find it.

Well, he'd been looking for the past hour, but so far, he'd found nothing to indicate that when Josie summoned the demon, Rick would have anything to fight him with—or fight him for.

"Approval for what?"

She shrugged. "I don't know. You tell me."

He knew what she was talking about. They hadn't talked directly about the confession he'd made to her back in the apartment in New York, but the specter of his admission had haunted them for days. He'd said his piece, but Josie had remained stone silent. "I don't need his permission to love you, Josie. I already told you I did," he snapped. "You're the one who didn't answer."

She zipped up the bag she'd used for the supplies and then skewered him with a sharp glare. "Yes, you did. But what exactly did you expect me to say in return?"

Rick groaned. Now wasn't the time or place for this conversation, though to be honest, they'd had plenty of more appropriate opportunities that neither of them had taken advantage of. Since the moment they'd found out that Father Tino was in Chicago, they'd spent every waking moment together on gathering information about the priest, the relic and the demon. They'd read everything in the library in the back room of Josie's store, which a friend had been running for Josie in her absence, and had even consulted Regina's aunt Marion, an elderly witch who apparently couldn't be bothered to remember to brush her shock of white hair, but who could recall in detail the contents of every single book in the library at a huge building called the Registry, a place where magical witches kept track of their kind. Now they only had to find out where the hand was. If, indeed, the good padre had it at all.

"Let's deal with this first," Rick suggested.

She clucked her tongue. "You've never seemed like the runaway-from-a-tough-situation kind of guy."

He stopped scanning the names of the interred for clues to the location of the hand and spun on her. "I'm not running from my feelings for you, Josie. You're the one who hasn't come within five feet of me since that night."

"I'm not into the whole 'friends with benefits' thing, sorry."

"What?"

"You said you loved me, but you couldn't make any promises. How convenient. And then you get mad because I cut off the free flow of sex. Why do you get to say how you feel and then put rules on how far those feelings go? What did you expect me to do? Jump into your arms and be happy for the little crumb you'd just thrown me?"

Rick blinked a few times, just to make sure he wasn't hallucinating or hearing things. But Josie was still standing there, her hands on her hips, her eyes challenging him. She'd lost her temper with him before, but this time it was different. Maybe because he was just as angry with himself as she was with him, but he could find no way to admit that without shredding his pride.

"I'm sorry if the truth isn't enough for you," he said.

"Is it enough for you?"

Rick's watch chimed, saving him from having to answer Josie's pointed question. They'd decided to perform the ceremony at two in the morning, when the moon was in the optimal position, according to Josie's reading of the entry in the book of shadows that had discussed summoning demons.

"It's time."

She glowered at him. "Rather deal with a demon than with me, huh?"

He cursed and turned off the flashlight. The priest had said the hand would appear when it was needed. Maybe this was where the faith part came in, because Rick wanted to end this nightmare tonight. He took a lighter from his pocket and helped Josie ignite the candles.

He stood directly at the top point of the star and waited while she scattered herbs around the altar. From her pocket, she took out three vials and poured the contents into bowls painted with symbols associated with the demon. The crescent moon. A bodiless hand. A ball of fire.

Then she started to chant.

At the very same time, Rick began to pray.

20

THE SUMMONS WAS ANSWERED almost immediately. The tall, blond man with the ink-black eyes that they'd seen in the warehouse materialized on the altar, looking momentarily disconcerted even as he glistened nude against the night. Josie, hands outstretched, continued to chant, but changed the incantation from one of calling to one of containment.

From her pocket, she extracted a second set of potions, mixtures she'd brewed herself under the watchful eye of Regina and Lilith's aunt, Marion. Josie had no idea if the liquid magic would work when she had no real magical power to back it up, but she had to trust the knowledge she'd studied so hard to gain. Her sense of which roots and oils worked best together, her talent for following recipes—and her intense desire to keep Rick alive so he would stop being so stubborn and she could admit that she loved him with every inch of her soul drove her to chant louder and with more conviction.

"You," Ruhin said to Rick, who was standing in front of him, chin high, but eyes searching everywhere. He held the modified Taser in one hand, but she knew he didn't want to use it. He needed the hand of St. Augustina to destroy the demon permanently. Any other weapon would simply delay this battle to another night, another place.

Josie took a chance to look around as well. Father Tino had insisted they'd find the hand when they most needed it. Well, as the demon began to stalk back and forth atop the altar, she figured their need was pretty high. And still, nothing.

"Yes, me," Rick replied. "You've been looking for me. Here I am."

Josie wanted to step around so she could see the demon's expression, but she continued chanting and remained where she was. For all she knew, she was the only thing keeping the demon from attacking.

"You are the one," the demon announced.

"The one who has been killing your minions and trying to smoke you out, yes, that's me," Rick verified.

He continued to chance glances with each taunt, buying time.

The demon laughed uproariously. "If you have summoned me, then you must have what I seek."

Rick held out his hands, the Taser clutched tightly. "And what exactly is that?"

Ruhin moved to step down from the altar but was blocked by Josie's spell. She exchanged a surprised look with Rick. She knew she'd done everything as instructed, but she hadn't been certain it was going to actually work.

"What holds me?" Ruhin demanded.

He twisted around on the altar, his blond hair and manly bits arcing with the rotation. He glared down at Josie, who had to close her own eyes to make sure she didn't miss a syllable. The manly bits she could ignore, but the stare? It was black with evil and bored straight into her. Did she have to continue speaking the chant to keep him contained? She wasn't sure, but she wasn't taking any chances.

"It's me you have to worry about," Rick shouted.

Josie peeked one eye open. Ruhin had turned.

"Were you the warlock Perkins Dafoe?" Rick asked.

"I've taken many names and invaded the bodies of many magical creatures for centuries, mundane."

"And now?" Rick asked.

The demon plucked at the skin on his bare chest.

"This mundane believed that taking his own life would spare his miserable existence, but he had not yet done the deed. Unlike you, he was open to the idea of limitless power and strength beyond measure. He chose me over death."

"Then are you human or demon?"

Josie watched the creature's chest and back ripple as he inhaled. His laughter as he exhaled cut straight through to her bones.

"We shall soon find out."

A second later, a blast rocked the mausoleum. Josie flew backward and landed hard against the marble wall. Pain shattered her concentration, and black spots blocked her vision. She blinked, trying to clear her eyes, scratching at the floor in an attempt to climb back to her feet, but she could not muster the balance or strength. She watched in horror as Ruhin jumped down from the altar, less than a foot away from Rick.

"No," she squeaked. She threw the potion in her left hand. The contents exploded just behind the demon in a flash of blue smoke.

Still unable to get up, Josie crawled on the floor, struggling to reach Rick when the bloodstone around her neck burned white-hot. She cursed. As if she needed a warning now? Wasn't it a little late this time? But at the same moment, her hand rolled over a tile in the floor that gave way, flipped upward and cut her forearm. She winced and blinked, trying to see what was happening. Then she noticed what lay inside the hole in the ground.

The hand of St. Augustina.

She wasn't as grossed-out as she'd prepared herself to be, as the hand was entombed in a tiny wooden casket carved with two hands folded in reverent prayer. She moved to take it from its resting place, but then remembered only the faithful could touch it. But faithful to what? She was betting that paganism wasn't much thought of by the good saint, so Josie closed the tile, shoved her hip atop it and shouted Rick's name.

Ruhin fought like a man—no energy bursts or magic— which told her he had indeed taken human form. Rick seemed to realize the same and had abandoned the Taser to do damage with his fists. He sported a jagged cut above his swollen eye that dripped blood down his cheek, but Ruhin looked just as bad. The demon's blond hair now hung in sweaty strings and his once-glistening chest was battered and bruised. Rick executed an impressive swinging kick, sent the demon skidding across the floor and then dove to her side.

"Are you—"

She answered the question by displacing the tile again. His eye lit on the prize inside, then he gazed on her with such intense relief, she knew he would have kissed her had there been time.

"I love you," he whispered.

She smiled and gulped down her excess of emotion. "I know."

He reached into the hole and snatched the casket just as the demon descended on them.

The creature's sharp-toothed grin turned Josie's stomach.

"At last," he said, grabbing for the casket. His fingers brushed the wood, but Rick, moving fast, gripped Josie and together, they rolled underneath the altar.

Josie threw the second potion, which exploded this time in a cloud of pure white. Rick pulled her behind a statue as the demon howled in frustration and pain.

"Here we go," Rick said. "It's now or never."

"Go get him," Josie encouraged, sparing a split second for a quick kiss.

Rick tore open the casket, grasped the hand by the wrist and held it toward the supernatural being. Josie's entire body shook with adrenaline and fear. She grabbed Rick's shoulder, needing to hold on to him. She tried not to look at the severed hand, but seconds before the mausoleum ignited with a golden gleam emanating from the fingertips, she saw how the hand still looked lovely and smooth, as if hundreds of years had not passed since it had been cut from its owner's arm.

Rick recited a prayer, something simple that she'd heard a thousand times. The demon dropped to his knees. The light became so bright Josie could no longer watch. She crouched behind Rick, pressed her chin to his back and repeated the chants for peace and tranquility she'd learned by heart, until a deafening boom rocked the marble building and then… *nothing.*

THE ACRID SMELL of burnt flesh clung to every fiber of his clothing, making Rick wince as he stripped from his jacket and wrapped it around Josie before he moved her out of the mausoleum and into the frigid cemetery air. Ash and dust followed them out of the tiny building and they coughed until their lungs and vision cleared.

Rick set Josie down near a gravestone. "You okay?"

She nodded, still coughing. "Fine. Is he—?"

"I think so. Wait here."

He went back inside, ignoring the sting in his eyes. Where the demon hybrid had stood moments before, there was nothing now but a deep indentation in the marble floor filled with grayish white ash and bits of bone. Rick said a quick prayer for what was left of the soul of the man who'd succumbed to the demon's invasion, then scooped the remains into an empty vase upturned in the battle, placed them underneath the loose tile and returned to the open air.

The hand, he noticed, had disappeared.

And so had his destiny.

For the first time since he was six years old, Rick realized that he no longer had the prophecy hanging over his head. Yes, the night was dark and his lungs burned with dust and cinders, but he'd never felt more clean. More free. He didn't have words to express the lightness in his heart, so he simply kissed Josie until she pulled back, placed her hands on his cheeks and stared intently into his eyes.

"What is it?"

"It's over," he replied. "It's finally over."

Wrapping his arm around Josie's waist, he spurred her across to the other side of the cemetery, where Father Tino was waiting for them, surprisingly, with Regina St. Lyon. He had a lot to say to Josie, but he needed time to find the right words. The priest and the witch, on the other hand, were sitting on a bench across from a tall statue of an angel ascending to the heavens, discussing, it seemed, the pagan imagery prevalent in the life-size work of religious art.

"And you see there," Regina said. "Those swirls on her belt? Those are called the Celtic triple spiral, each representing a phase of the—"

Rick coughed and instantly they both jumped to their feet. Father Tino grabbed Josie and helped Rick take her to the bench while Regina disappeared, then reappeared seconds later with dust clinging to her indigo robes.

Josie started coughing again, but slapped their hands aside and insisted she was fine. "I'm not dying, for Pete's sake!"

"You know that expression refers to St. Peter, yes?" Father Tino admonished with more than a hint of humor.

"Yes, Father, I do," Josie said with a smile. "At this point, I'll take an intervention from whoever will give it to me."

The priest nodded approvingly. "I've found that always to be a logical policy. The demon is gone?"

Regina drew Josie into an embrace. "Crater that size? Yes,

he's gone. For good. I can't feel his presence anywhere."
Regina turned to Rick. "I'll check with the council, of course,
but I believe you and Josie accomplished your task."

Rick rolled his eyes at Regina's formal speech, but then
decided that despite her regal manner and air of self-importance,
she wasn't so bad. She had helped Josie with the potions and
those bursts of magical energy had given him the split-second
advantage he'd needed to take the demon down.

Father Tino pounded him on the back.

"How are you going to explain that mess?" Rick asked,
nodding toward the mausoleum across the cemetery, which
was still smoldering, wisps of smoke swirling into the frigid
February air.

"Vándalos," the priest answered quickly. "Terrible how
these things happen. But I should return to the rectory before
I'm missed. Your confrontation was not quiet. You should all
leave as soon as possible."

They exited the cemetery and at the gate that led in one
direction to the church and in the other to the front street,
Father Tino made Rick promise to attend mass soon. He
then turned to Regina.

"It was very interesting to meet you," Father Tino said, his
tone sincere.

Regina gave the priest a little bow. "The same with you.
Though I suspect, if these two ever get around to concentrating on themselves now that all the demons and warlocks and
such are taken care of, I'll see you again very soon."

She walked into a nearby copse of trees in the courtyard
and faded from view.

"Did she just—" the priest asked Rick.

"Best not to think too much about it, Father. It hurts the brain."

"Was she right? Will I be seeing her again, possibly to celebrate a happier occasion?"

Rick glanced at Josie, whose hair was a mess, her face smudged with dirt, smelling of smoke and burnt spearmint. She'd wandered to the sidewalk in the front of the church and settled onto a bench at the bus stop, making Rick wonder suddenly how they were going to get home.

"You'll be the first to know, Padre," he promised, then left to join her.

He would have worried more about getting a ride if he had any clue where they were going to go. They'd been staying at her place, in the apartment where, six months ago, he'd first realized she was a Wiccan and where he'd first resisted the incredible pull of their mutual attraction. He had not returned to his own apartment in case Ruhin had the place staked out. But now, with the demon gone for good, he could go back.

But he did not want to.

He wanted to stay with Josie. And not just for the night. She'd been his light in this shadow of a life he'd been living since his first run-in with Ruhin. Now, with the demon gone, he wanted her more than ever. But would she feel the same now that her sense of obligation had been fulfilled?

He slid into the space beside Josie and, not caring how she reacted, slipped his hand into hers.

"It's over," he said.

She took a deep breath and then exhaled, announcing brightly, "Yes, it is."

"How long do you think I should wait before I admit I was an idiot?"

Josie glanced at him from the corner of her eye. "Oh, I think you've waited quite long enough."

He twisted around, noting the setting and atmosphere. He supposed there were better places to beg a woman's forgiveness and pledge undying love, maybe even throw in a marriage proposal, than in front of a church in the dead of night. But they weren't going anywhere anytime soon and as she'd said, he'd waited long enough to admit that his way of expressing his feelings for her before hadn't been up to scratch.

"Josie, I'm an idiot."

She turned and took his other hand, her blue eyes sparkling with humor. "That's a good start. Short, sweet and to the point. Go on," she urged.

"I don't deserve you," he said.

She nodded. "Also true. Keep going."

"But I love you more than I've ever loved anyone in my entire life. For the past six months, I couldn't imagine any future peaceful enough for a real relationship. Now, I can't imagine any future that doesn't have you."

She blinked rapidly and shifted in her seat, sniffling as if something was suddenly tickling her nose.

"I shouldn't have just clammed up when you said you loved me," she admitted. "I've never had anyone tell me that before. I guess I had a pretty high ideal of how that particular moment would go down, and I'm pretty sure I never thought it would happen just after I'd suffered a head injury on account of a naked demon."

Rick laughed loud and hard, feeling humor through every nerve ending for the first time in forever. Josie joined in and the sound unleashed even more of his happiness. He couldn't help swallowing her up in a hug, pressing her face to his chest and tilting his chin over top, cocooning them in an embrace of pure mirth and release.

But after a minute, moisture soaked his shirt and he realized that she was crying.

"Josie, what's wrong?"

She looked up at him, her eyes red and increasingly puffy, her lips moist and plump and delectable. "I still haven't worked up how to tell you I love you. And it's Valentine's Day."

Rick had to stop and think. They'd been so wrapped up in the little matter of defeating a demon, he'd totally forgotten what day of the week it was, much less some holiday. Besides, did it matter? Josie had just said, without actually *saying,* that she loved him. He hooked his finger around the chain Josie wore and tugged the bloodstone free.

"Call Regina," he said.

"What?"

"Do it."

She complied and seconds later, Regina St. Lyon stood in front of them again, her arms crossed impatiently around her middle and her husband, Brock Aegis, standing behind her half-undressed and looking incredibly annoyed.

"You rang?" Regina asked.

Rick caught Josie's eye. Apparently, they'd interrupted Regina's romantic interlude with her husband, judging by the little red cupid tattoo on Brock's rather impressive pec.

"Just wondering if you could give us a ride," Josie said.

"Where to?"

"Home," Rick replied, realizing he did know exactly where that was—wherever Josie was.

Josie snuggled tighter to him and whispered, "My place."

The sensation of being magically transported across the city was nothing compared to the feeling of Josie clinging to him as if her life depended on it. When the rush of wind dispersed, he opened his eyes to find himself standing in the middle of Josie's living room.

Only it didn't look like the living room they'd left that evening. Every spare surface had been covered with thick, red candles and the scents of rose blossom and cinnamon hung exotically in the air.

"Who—"

"Me," Josie said. "With some help from my very magical

friends. It may not be a Wiccan holiday, but under the circumstances, I thought we should celebrate Valentine's Day the right way."

Rick pulled Josie closer, though if they pressed any more tightly together, they'd be sharing one body. Which, come to think of it, was an excellent idea.

"It is the first day of our new life. Not my new life and your new life, but ours. Together. I love you, Josie," he said. "Last week, chasing a demon I was destined to destroy, I wasn't sure I'd live. Now, I'm just certain I don't want to live without you."

"I can't live without you," she replied. "I love you. I think I always have." Josie braced her hands on either side of his cheeks and drew him into a kiss that seemed to make the flames of the candles around them flare with both heat and happiness. Their clothes peeled away, they ended up in her tiny bathroom, surrounded by the steam of a scalding shower that washed away the signs of the battle. By the time they were dry and standing again in the warm and fragrant living room, they were naked, clean and anxious to begin the normal life they'd put off for entirely too long.

Rick dropped to his knees and placed a possessive kiss on Josie's thigh.

"Now what do we do?" he asked.

"Now that we've saved the world and admitted we love each other?" Josie replied wryly, her fingers streaming through his thick, damp hair. "Do you really have to ask?"

Rick chuckled, pulled Josie to her knees beside him and murmured against her lips, "Let's start with something wicked."

* * * * *

*Harlequin is 60 years old,
and Harlequin Blaze is celebrating!
After all, a lot can happen in 60 years, or 60 minutes…or
60 seconds!
Find out what's going down in
Blaze's heart-stopping new mini-series,*
FROM 0 TO 60!
*Getting from "Hello" to "How was it?"
can happen fast….*

Here's a sneak peek of the first book,
A LONG, HARD RIDE
by Alison Kent
Available March 2009

"Is that for me?" Trey asked.

Cardin Worth cocked her head to the side and considered how much better the day already seemed. "Good morning to you, too."

When she didn't hold out the second cup of coffee for him to take, he came closer. She sipped from her heavy white mug, hiding her grin and her giddy rush of nerves behind it.

But when he stopped in front of her, she made the mistake of lowering her gaze from his face to the exposed strip of his chest. It was either give him his cup of coffee or bury her nose against him and breathe in. She remembered so clearly how he smelled. How he tasted.

She gave him his coffee.

After taking a quick gulp, he smiled and said, "Good morning, Cardin. I hope the floor wasn't too hard for you."

The hardness of the floor hadn't been the problem. She shook her head. "Are you kidding? I slept like a baby, swaddled in my sleeping bag."

"In my sleeping bag, you mean."

If he wanted to get technical, yeah. "Thanks for the loaner. It made sleeping on the floor almost bearable." As had the warmth of his spooned body, she thought, then quickly changed the subject. "I saw you have a loaf of bread and some eggs. Would you like me to cook breakfast?"

He lowered his coffee mug slowly, his gaze as warm as the sun on her shoulders, as the ceramic heating her hands. "I didn't bring you out here to wait on me."

"You didn't bring me out here at all. I volunteered to come."

"To help me get ready for the race. Not to serve me."

"It's just breakfast, Trey. And coffee." Even if last night it had been more. Even if the way he was looking at her made her want to climb back into that sleeping bag. "I work much better when my stomach's not growling. I thought it might be the same for you."

"It is, but I'll cook. You made the coffee."

"That's because I can't work at all without caffeine."

"If I'd known that, I would've put on a pot as soon I got up."

"What time *did* you get up?" Judging by the sun's position, she swore it couldn't be any later than seven now. And, yeah, they'd agreed to start working at six.

"Maybe four?" he guessed, giving her a lazy smile.

"But it was almost two…" She let the sentence dangle, finishing the thought privately. She was quite sure he knew exactly what time they'd finally fallen asleep after he'd made love to her.

The question facing her now was where did this relationship—if you could even call it *that*—go from here?

* * * * *

*Cardin and Trey are about to find
out that great sex is only the beginning….
Don't miss the fireworks!*

*Get ready for
A LONG, HARD RIDE
by Alison Kent
Available March 2009,
wherever Blaze books are sold.*

CELEBRATE
60 YEARS
OF PURE READING PLEASURE
WITH HARLEQUIN®!

**We'll be spotlighting a different series
every month throughout 2009
to celebrate our 60th anniversary.**

Look for Harlequin® Blaze™ in March!

O-6O

*After all, a lot can happen in 60 years,
or 60 minutes...or 60 seconds!*

Find out what's going down in Blaze's
heart-stopping new miniseries *0-60!*
Getting from "Hello" to "How was it?"
can happen fast....

Look for the brand-new 0-60 miniseries in March 2009!

www.eHarlequin.com   HBRIDE09

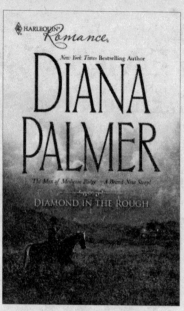

DIAMOND IN THE ROUGH

John Callister is a millionaire rancher, yet when he meets lovely Sassy Peale and she thinks he's a cowboy, he goes along with her misconception. He's had enough of gold diggers, and this is a chance to be valued for himself, not his money. But when Sassy finds out the truth, she feels John was merely playing with her. John will have to convince her that he's truly the man she fell in love with—a diamond in the rough.

THE MEN OF MEDICINE RIDGE—a brand-new miniseries set in the wilds of Montana!

Available April 2009 wherever you buy books.

www.eHarlequin.com

HR17577

HARLEQUIN Romance

This February the Harlequin® Romance series
will feature six Diamond Brides stories featuring
diamond proposals and gorgeous grooms.

Share your dream wedding proposal and you could WIN!

The most romantic entry will win a diamond
necklace and will inspire a proposal in one of
our upcoming Diamond Grooms books in 2010.

In 100 words or less, tell us the most romantic
way that you dream of being proposed to.

For more information, and to enter
the Diamond Brides Proposal contest, please visit
www.DiamondBridesProposal.com

Or mail your entry to us at:

IN THE U.S.: 3010 Walden Ave., P.O. Box 9069, Buffalo, NY 14269-9069
IN CANADA: 225 Duncan Mill Road, Don Mills, ON M3B 3K9

REQUEST YOUR FREE BOOKS!

2 FREE NOVELS
PLUS 2
FREE GIFTS!

HARLEQUIN®

Blaze™

Red-hot reads!

YES! Please send me 2 FREE Harlequin® Blaze™ novels and my 2 FREE gifts (gifts are worth about $10). After receiving them, if I don't wish to receive any more books, I can return the shipping statement marked "cancel". If I don't cancel, I will receive 6 brand-new novels every month and be billed just $4.24 per book in the U.S. or $4.71 per book in Canada, plus 25¢ shipping and handling per book and applicable taxes, if any*. That's a savings of 15% or more off the cover price! I understand that accepting the 2 free books and gifts places me under no obligation to buy anything. I can always return a shipment and cancel at any time. Even if I never buy another book, the two free books and gifts are mine to keep forever.

151 HDN ERVA   351 HDN ERUX

Name _____ (PLEASE PRINT) _____

Address _____ Apt. # _____

City _____ State/Prov. _____ Zip/Postal Code _____

Signature (if under 18, a parent or guardian must sign)

Mail to the **Harlequin Reader Service:**
IN U.S.A.: P.O. Box 1867, Buffalo, NY 14240-1867
IN CANADA: P.O. Box 609, Fort Erie, Ontario L2A 5X3

Not valid to current subscribers of Harlequin Blaze books.

Want to try two free books from another line?
Call 1-800-873-8635 or visit www.morefreebooks.com.

* Terms and prices subject to change without notice. N.Y. residents add applicable sales tax. Canadian residents will be charged applicable provincial taxes and GST. Offer not valid in Quebec. This offer is limited to one order per household. All orders subject to approval. Credit or debit balances in a customer's account(s) may be offset by any other outstanding balance owed by or to the customer. Please allow 4 to 6 weeks for delivery. Offer available while quantities last.

Your Privacy: Harlequin Books is committed to protecting your privacy. Our Privacy Policy is available online at www.eHarlequin.com or upon request from the Reader Service. From time to time we make our lists of customers available to reputable third parties who may have a product or service of interest to you. If you would prefer we not share your name and address, please check here. ☐

HB08R

You're invited to join our Tell Harlequin Reader Panel!

By joining our new reader panel you will:

- Receive Harlequin® books—they are FREE and yours to keep with no obligation to purchase anything!
- Participate in fun online surveys
- Exchange opinions and ideas with women just like you
- Have a say in our new book ideas and help us publish the best in women's fiction

In addition, you will have a chance to win great prizes and receive special gifts! See Web site for details. Some conditions apply. Space is limited.

To join, visit us at

www.TellHarlequin.com.

COMING NEXT MONTH
Available February 10, 2009

#453 A LONG, HARD RIDE Alison Kent
From 0–60
All Cardin Worth wants is to put her broken family together again. And if that means seducing Trey Davis, her first love, well, a girl's got to do what a girl's got to do. Only, she never expected to enjoy it quite so much....

#454 UP CLOSE AND DANGEROUSLY SEXY Karen Anders
Drew Miller's mission: train a fellow agent's twin sister to replace her in a sting op. Expect the unexpected is his mantra, but he never anticipated that his trainee, Allie Carpenter, would be teaching him a thing or twelve in the bedroom!

#455 ONCE AN OUTLAW Debbi Rawlins
Stolen from Time, Bk. 1
Sam Watkins has a past he's trying to forget. Reese Winslow is desperate to remember a way home. Caught in the Old West, they share an intensely passionate affair that has them joining forces. But does that mean they'll be together forever?

#456 STILL IRRESISTIBLE Dawn Atkins
Years ago Callie Cummings and Declan O'Neill had an unforgettable fling. And now she's back in town. He's still tempting, still irresistible, and she can't get images of him and tangled sheets out of her mind. The only solution? An unforgettable fling, round two.

#457 ALWAYS READY Joanne Rock
Uniformly Hot!
Lieutenant Damon Craig has always tried to live up to the Coast Guard motto: Always Ready. But when sexy sociologist Lacey Sutherland stumbles into a stakeout, alerting his suspects—and his libido—Damon knows he doesn't stand a chance....

#458 BODY CHECK Elle Kennedy
When sexually frustrated professor Hayden Houston meets hot hockey star Brody Croft in a bar, she's ready for a one-night stand. But can Brody convince Hayden that he's good for more than just a body check?

www.eHarlequin.com

HBCNMBPA0209